A D███ ██se

By
Henrik Ibsen

An Acting Version by
Thornton Wilder

A SAMUEL FRENCH ACTING EDITION

SAMUEL
FRENCH
FOUNDED 1830

SAMUELFRENCH.COM
SAMUELFRENCH-LONDON.CO.UK

ISBN 978-0-573-70526-7

www.SamuelFrench.com
www.SamuelFrench-London.co.uk

A DOLL'S HOUSE was first produced by Mr. Jed Harris at the Morosco Theatre in New York City on December 27, 1937. The performance was directed by Jed Harris with scenic and costume desgin by Donald Oenslager, choreography by Martha Graham, music by Bernice Richmond, women's costumes by Helene Pons, men's costumes by Eaves, shoes by Israel Miller. The scenery was built by Vail Construction Company and painted by Robert W. Bergman, Inc., the electrical equipment was by Century Lighting; the technical assistant to Mr. Oenslager was Isaac Benesch, the general manager was Joe Glick, the press representative was Emanuel Eisenberg, the assistant on production was Harold Johnsrud, the master carpenter was Frank Dwyer, the master electrician was Thomas Connel and the master of properties was Max Davis. The cast was as follows:

THORWALD HELMER . . . . Dennis King

NORA HELMER . . . . Ruth Gordon

EMMY . . . . Lorna Lynn Meyers

IVAR . . . . Howard Sherman

DOCTOR RANK . . . . Paul Lukas

CHRISTINA LINDEN . . . . Margaret Waller

NILS KROGSTAD . . . . Sam Jaffe

ANNA . . . . Grace Mills

ELLEN . . . . Jessica Rogers

PORTER . . . . Harold Johnsrud

A DOLL'S HOUSE was presented by Theatre for a New Audience (Jeffrey Horowitz, Artistic Director; Henry Christensen III, Chairman; Dorothy Ryan, Managing Director) at the Polonsky Shakespeare Center in Brooklyn, New York, on May 22, 2016. The production was directed by Arin Arbus, the scenic designer was Riccardo Hernandez, the costume designer was Susan Hilferty, the lighting designer was Marcus Doshi, the choreographer was Sam Pinkleton, the composer/co-sound designer was Daniel Kluger, the co-sound designer was Lee Kinney, the hair and makeup designer was Dave Bova, the properties supervisor was Jon Knust, the dramaturg was Jonathan Kalb, the fight director was J. Allen Suddeth, casting was by Deborah Brown, the production stage manager was Diane Healy, the assistant stage managers were Anne Ciarlone and Tori Sheehan, the press representative was The Bruce Cohen Group and the general manager was Michael Page. The cast was as follows:

THORWALD HELMER	John Douglas Thompson
NORA HELMER	Maggie Lacey
EMMY	Jayla Lavender Nicholas
IVAR	Ruben Almash
DOCTOR RANK	Nigel Gore
CHRISTINA LINDEN	Linda Powell
NILS KROGSTAD	Jesse J. Perez
ANNA	Laurie Kennedy
ELLEN	Kimber Monroe
PORTER	Christian J. Mallen

CHARACTERS

THORWALD HELMER
NORA HELMER – Helmer's wife
EMMY – their daughter
IVAR – their son
DOCTOR RANK
CHRISTINA LINDEN
NILS KROGSTAD
ANNA – the nurse
ELLEN – the maid
PORTER

SETTING

The action takes place in Helmer's house.

ACT I

(The home of Thorwald **HELMER**, *an honest member of the middle class, in Norway, late in the nineteenth century.)*

(It is a pleasant warm, conventional, comfortable room, an adequate shelter for a wife, a growing reputation, and a pair of children. On stage left, double windows and a stove are guarantees against the northern cold. On stage right a glassed-in corridor leads from the outer door directly to **HELMER***'s study, passing other doors to the dining room and kitchen. In the rear wall are a pair of identical double doors, revealing, when they open, on the left,* **NORA***'s room, with the nursery beyond; on the right,* **HELMER***'s study.)*

(The room is furnished, for its time, simply. There is a splendid square piano center, and above it hang pictures, collected variously during eight years of marriage and probably not too closely regarded now. The piano is flanked by walnut side-chairs, relatives of two matching sofas, downstage right, with a small low table between them. Double doors, stage right, open in the center of the glassed-in wall. Stage left there are two windows, opening on the street, one story below. Between them stands the great stove, symbol of the secure comfort of the house. There are pleasant lamps of the period on a small table up left of the piano. There are small side tables beside a deep chair left, and to the right of the two matching sofas. There is a larger oval, inlaid table, up right, with a hanging shelf of books above it. There is some, but not too much,

bric-a-brac, and on the piano some books of old tunes.)

*(It is winter, the day before Christmas; the afternoon light is dying, casting shadows on the floor, the room is empty. The doors to **HELMER**'s study are closed; at the left, half of the doors to **NORA**'s room are slightly ajar. There is a short loud peal on the doorbell to the flat, then another, longer one. After a moment the maid, **ELLEN**, comes from her kitchen quarters, up left in the corridor, to open the door.)*

NORA. *(Out of sight at the door.)* Oh, thank you, Ellen. You'd better help me.

*(Her arms loaded with packages gaily wrapped, **NORA** surrenders some of them to **ELLEN**, shoves open the doors, stage left center, and sweeps into the room. Behind her is the **PORTER**, a basket of more parcels in one hand, a toy horse under one arm, a Christmas tree in his only remaining hand.)*

NORA. You bring that in here. How much?

PORTER. Oh, whatever you like, ma'am. A few pennies will do.

*(He sets down the tree, **NORA** takes the basket, he leaves the horse on the sofa.)*

NORA. Here!

*(She gives him a coin, takes up a box of flowers and crosses to the piano bench with them. **ELLEN** has set down some of the packages on the oval table. The **PORTER** fumbles for change.)*

Oh, no, keep the change. Merry Christmas!

PORTEr. Thank you, ma'am. Merry Christmas to you.

*(He exits, cap in hand, as **NORA** quickly undoes the flowers.)*

ELLEN. Oh…flowers, too, ma'am!

NORA. Yes, Ellen, and so awfully expensive!

ELLEN. Well, they'll need some water. I'll go fetch a vase.

(She starts out for the kitchen.)

NORA. Yes, Ellen...hurry! Oh, are the children home yet?

ELLEN. No, ma'am. They're still out with Anna.

NORA. Oh! Come and take the tree into the kitchen...they mustn't see it until tonight.

*(**ELLEN** returns to the room. She picks up the tree, starts out with it.)*

ELLEN. Yes, ma'am. I understand. Mr. Helmer's got home already. He's in his study.

(She exits with the tree, through the vestibule, into the kitchen.)

NORA. Oh...

*(**NORA** listens an instant at **HELMER**'s door, begins to remove her gloves, coat and hat. She whistles a pleasant, gay little tune.)*

HELMER. *(At his desk, inside the study, behind the doors.)* Is that you, Nora?

NORA. *(Pushing open the double doors to his study and hurrying up to his desk.)* Oh, Thorwald, I'm so glad you're at home. Come here! Come see what I've bought. The most wonderful bargains!

HELMER. My dear, I wish you wouldn't interrupt me.

NORA. Do come here!

*(At this moment **ELLEN** has come out of the kitchen with a vase, crossed the vestibule, and entered the room. **NORA** runs merrily out of the study, taking the vase.)*

Oh, thank you, Ellen...give that to me.

*(**ELLEN** turns to exit, sees the toy horse, bravely standing on the sofa right.)*

ELLEN. Well, well...

NORA. *(Already at the piano, arranging her flowers.)* Oh, yes, that's a horse.

(**ELLEN** *smiles and exits to the kitchen.*)

Do come here, Thorwald!

(**HELMER**, *disturbed at his work, must perforce rise, and he now saunters into the living room.*)

Darling, you should see the tree! It's the most wonderful bargain.

HELMER. (*Surveying the litter of packages.*) You mean to say you've bought all these?

NORA. Oh, just a few little things. For the children...and Ellen and Anna...and Doctor Rank.

HELMER. (*He picks up one of the packages, then examines another.*) How many toys does it take to amuse these children?

NORA. (*Flies down, taking the package from him, hiding it swiftly under the chair left of the piano.*) No, no, not that one! You mustn't see that till tonight.

HELMER. (*Indulgently going to close the doors to the vestibule.*) Mmmm... I suppose you spent every penny I gave you.

NORA. (*Back again at her flowers.*) No, I did have some left... and then I saw these heavenly roses.

HELMER. (*Strolling toward the stove.*) But that's extravagant, my dear.

NORA. I know, Thorwald, I know. I just couldn't resist them.

HELMER. What a creature, what a creature.

(*He picks up his pipe, laid ready for him on the side table, and strikes a match for it.*)

And what did you buy for yourself?

NORA. Oh, I don't need anything.

HELMER. Nonsense. Tell me what you'd like.

NORA. Not a single thing.

HELMER. Put your little mind to it. Something useful... sensible.

NORA. Well...

HELMER. (*Back to her, still puffing his pipe to light it.*) Mmm?

NORA. If you really do want to give me something...You haven't bought anything yet, have you? *(She half turns toward him.)*

HELMER. No, I've been too busy at the bank.

NORA. Well, look, dearest...you could give me money!

HELMER. Now, Nora!

NORA. *(With a graceful, childlike blandness, she crosses toward him.)* And then I could buy myself something...just what I needed.

HELMER. There's no Christmas spirit about cold, hard money.

NORA. Oh, yes there is!

HELMER. But you're so extravagant, my dear. And we simply can't afford to go throwing money about, you know.

NORA. I know, but you'll be making lots of money now. Surely we can throw it about a little!

HELMER. My dear, my job doesn't even start till after New Year's.

NORA. *(Directly behind him, her hands placatingly on his shoulders.)* That's only next week.

HELMER. And I have to wait a whole quarter for my first check.

NORA. I know, but we can borrow enough in the meantime. We can get lots of credit now.

HELMER. *(Now touched on a vital point, he turns toward her for the first time.)* Borrow? My dear child, have you ever known me to borrow money?

NORA. No, but it ought to be easy enough now.

HELMER. I want no creditors in my life, thank you. We've held out all these years without ever owing anyone a penny, and we're certainly not going to begin now at the last minute.

NORA. Yes, darling...

HELMER. Besides, it would look bad...a man in my position.

NORA. *(Patting him soothingly, she moves away toward the sofas.)* Yes, I suppose so. Of course you know best, Thorwald.

HELMER. *(Relenting a little, now that he has gained his point.)* At the same time, we're not exactly paupers. It's a comfort to know we've lived within our means...no debts to worry us.

> *(He sits in his deep chair, left.)*

NORA. *(Busily prying into one of her purchases, at the table, right.)* Yes, darling.

HELMER. I've even managed to save a little. Not many men could have done that, on my salary.

NORA. *(Piling some of her parcels on top of the others.)* No, Thorwald.

HELMER. *(In a mood for largesse, he draws out his wallet.)* And things are getting a little easier. Well, after all... Nora, what do you think I've got here?

NORA. *(Turning around instantly and racing to him.)* Money!

HELMER. *(Pulling out a handful of notes.)* I know you've been looking forward to Christmas...

NORA. *(Just behind him, she reaches out with both hands and takes what currency she can.)* Ten, twenty, thirty, forty...

HELMER. *(Clutching the funds to him.)* Here, here...

NORA. *(Hurrying into her room before he can change his mind.)* Oh, Thorwald, thank you! This will go a long way!

> *(We hear a drawer slam, as she caches the money in her bureau.)*

HELMER. I should hope so. No one would believe how much it costs a man to keep a little thing like you.

NORA. *(Bustling back into the room to get her packages out of sight.)* Even little things have expenses, Thorwald.

HELMER. Just like your father...reaching out for money, money, all the time.

> *(**NORA** takes an armload of presents into her room.)*

HELMER. Still, it's certainly a cheerier Christmas this year than last.

NORA. *(Back in the living room to dispose of more packages.)* Mmmmm.

HELMER. I hardly saw you at all, remember? You shut yourself up in your room, toiling over those homemade decorations. Lord, I was bored.

> *(**NORA** has gone into her room with the last of her presents. She now returns and moves to the side of **THORWALD**'s chair, ready for something that has long been on her mind.)*

NORA. Well, I wasn't. Look, Thorwald, I thought...

> *(She sits down on a small side chair, left of Thorwald's easy chair, when the doorbell rings.)*

Oh, dear, company...what a bore!

> *(**ELLEN** enters the vestibule from the kitchen, goes to the front door.)*

Well, look, Thorwald, I think we ought to manage things a little differently now. After Christmas is over...

> *(But **ELLEN** has opened the glass doors, left center, as the figure of a man is seen passing behind her, entering **HELMER**'s study.)*

ELLEN. A lady to see you, Mrs. Helmer...

NORA. *(Rising.)* Oh, tell her to come in.

> *(**HELMER** rises.)*

ELLEN. *(Crossing to the piano for the emptied flower box.)* And Doctor Rank has gone into the study, Mr. Helmer.

HELMER. *(Crossing right and up to his study.)* I'll join him. Excuse me, Nora.

> *(He closes his study doors after him. **NORA** stands uncertainly, center. **ELLEN** exits into the vestibule with the flower box, and shows in the visitor, closing the left center doors behind her, and exiting. This is **CHRISTINA LINDEN**, who comes in smiling and is stopped by the look of puzzled unrecognition in **NORA**'s face.)*

MRS. LINDEN. How are you, Nora?

NORA. How do you do?

MRS. LINDEN. You don't remember me, do you?

NORA. I… I don't think I…

> (**CHRISTINA** *smiles again, uncertainly. Some remembered thing returns to* **NORA**'s *mind, and she rushes into her old friend's arms.*)

Why, yes! Christina! Is it really you?

MRS. LINDEN. It really is.

NORA. Christina! And to think I didn't even know you! But you're so changed, Christina! You're so…

MRS. LINDEN. *(As the two women hold each other, studying the changes time puts in the face.)* Yes, I guess I am. In nine or ten years…

NORA. Good heavens! Has it been as long as that? I just can't believe it!

> (**NORA** *hugs* **CHRISTINA** *heartily.*)

But what are you doing in town?

MRS. LINDEN. I arrived on the morning boat.

NORA. Oh! To spend Christmas. How wonderful! Do take your things off.

> (*She helps her off with her coat.*)

Aren't you frozen? Come, sit by the fire and be cozy.

> (*She moves her to* **HELMER**'s *big chair, left.*)

Yes, now I begin to see the sweet old face…it was only at the first glance I didn't…

> (*Quickly she puts* **CHRISTINA**'s *things on the chair by the piano and comes down to the footstool beside her.*)

Oh, what a thoughtless wretch I am! Oh, darling, how can you forgive me?

MRS. LINDEN. Forgive you?

NORA. Oh Christina! I forgot that you…

MRS. LINDEN. *(With no trace of sentiment.)* Yes, my husband died three years ago.

NORA. I saw it in the paper, but…Well, you know how it is. You must believe me, Christina, I meant to write to you, but somehow things kept distracting me, getting in the way, and… *(In a characteristically swift change of direction.)* Did he leave you anything?

MRS. LINDEN. Nothing.

NORA. Not even any children?

MRS. LINDEN. No.

NORA. Nothing? Not anything?

MRS. LINDEN. Not even a regret.

NORA. But what do you mean, Christina? How could you have…

MRS. LINDEN. Oh, it happens that way sometimes, Nora.

NORA. Darling, you must tell me the whole story. I never would have dreamed it! It must have been awful…and to be absolutely alone afterwards! You know I have two of the sweetest children, just wait till you see them! They're out with their nurse now. So there's nothing to disturb us and you can tell me all about it.

MRS. LINDEN. No dear, you tell me.

NORA. No, really, darling, I won't be selfish today, I'll just think of you.

MRS. LINDEN. *(Smiling at her friend's eagerness.)* Thank you, Nora.

NORA. Oh, but I must tell you one thing! Or have you heard of our wonderful luck?

MRS. LINDEN. No, what is it?

NORA. Just think, darling! My husband has been appointed manager of the savings bank!

MRS. LINDEN. He has? How splendid!

NORA. He starts his new position right after New Year's, with a great big wonderful salary, and a share of the profits… Oh, Christina, can you imagine how it makes you feel to have lots of money?

MRS. LINDEN. *(A little wistfully.)* It would certainly be nice to have what you need.

NORA. No only what you need, but heaps of money!... Heaps, my dear!

MRS. LINDEN. *(Laughing.)* Oh, Nora, Nora! You're just the same, you haven't changed a bit, you're still the same old spend-thrift!

NORA. But don't be ridiculous. I've had to work.

> *(She rises, goes up to the piano, rummages in her bag.)*

MRS. LINDEN. You? Work?

NORA. Yes, work! Sewing, embroidery, things like that. Other work, too! Oh yes, Thorwald hasn't been the only one.

> *(She takes a small striped sack from her bag, and plunges her hand in it, coming out with one of her little vices—macaroons.)*

Have one?

> *(CHRISTINA smiles and shakes her head. NORA crams a macaroon in her mouth and goes right on talking.)*

Of course, the poor darling has had a terrible time ever since we were married. He had to take on all sorts of odd jobs and work like a slave from morning till night. Well, it was just too much for him, and he became terribly ill. So then the doctors said he had to give up everything and go south.

> *(She is back again on the footstool.)*

MRS. LINDEN. It must have cost a terrible lot!

NORA. Seventeen hundred...wasn't that frightful!

MRS. LINDEN. What luck that you had it!

NORA. *(With the slightest of hesitations.)* Yes...we got it from Papa.

MRS. LINDEN. Oh...so you inherited?

NORA. Yes, Christina.

MRS. LINDEN. But your husband... I thought when I came in your maid announced the doctor.

NORA. Oh, Doctor Rank, yes... But he doesn't come as a doctor, he's our best friend. No, Thorwald hasn't had an hour's illness since then. And the children are so sturdy and so am I. Oh, Christina, here I keep talking about myself, just rattling on. Darling, tell me, is it really true that you didn't love him?

MRS. LINDEN. What?

NORA. Your husband. Didn't you really? Whatever could you have been thinking of? To marry him, I mean. Was it...was he rich?

MRS. LINDEN. Nora, do you realize I had to provide for three people? I simply had to find some means of support. But my husband's business fell to pieces when he died, and I was right back where I started from.

NORA. *(With the astonishment of a sheltered woman.)* But what did you do?

MRS. LINDEN. *(Matter-of-factly, without self-pity.)* Oh, I taught school, kept a shop, anything. It's all past now, Nora... Then, Mother died and my brothers grew up. That's why I couldn't stay in that town any longer. There was nothing to hold me there. You see, if I had something to keep me busy...I don't care what. Clerical work, something in an office, anything. Nora, when you told me just now about your good fortune, really! I was thinking of myself more than I was of you.

NORA. How do you mean?

MRS. LINDEN. Well, with your husband...a bank official...

NORA. Oh, I see! You mean perhaps Thorwald might be able to do something for you. Darling, that's a wonderful idea! I'll be so happy to help you!

> *(She rises, her busy mind already occupied with ways and means.)*

Now don't you worry about it another instant! *(Walking*

around slowly, a strategy taking shape.) Leave it all to me. First, I'll think of something pleasant to put him in a good humor, then I'll lead up to it... Oh, don't worry, I'll do it very, very skillfully!

MRS. LINDEN. Oh, Nora, it'll mean so much to me; you don't know how desperate I've been, you've never had to face such things.

NORA. *(Wisely, secretly.)* Don't you be so sure about that, my dear.

MRS. LINDEN. Oh, well, a little fancy work and so forth. You're a mere child, Nora.

NORA. Look here, Christina, don't you go patronizing me!

MRS. LINDEN. But, darling, I envy you.

NORA. You're just like everybody else. You all think I'm not fit for anything serious...

MRS. LINDEN. Well...

NORA. As if I hadn't had my share of troubles.

MRS. LINDEN. My dear Nora, you've just told me all your troubles.

NORA. *(Softly, as if debating whether to tell her.)* Oh, those things! I haven't told you my real troubles.

MRS. LINDEN. Your real troubles?

NORA. I know you look down on me, Christina. But you haven't any right to.

MRS. LINDEN. I'm sure I don't look down on anyone.

NORA. You're so proud of having taken care of your mother, aren't you? And of...

> *(The two women are practically talking at once now.)*

MRS. LINDEN. I'm glad that I had the...

NORA. And of your brothers, too! So proud that...

MRS. LINDEN. Don't I have the right to be proud?

NORA. You're not the only one!

MRS. LINDEN. I didn't say I was.

NORA. Let me tell you...I have something to be proud of, too.

MRS. LINDEN. I'm sure you have.

NORA. Well, I have. Shhh!

> *(A quick glance at* **HELMER***'s closed door, then she comes down again to the footstool.)*

Thorwald mustn't hear this for the world!

MRS. LINDEN. What on earth do you mean?

NORA. Listen, nobody knows about this…not anybody. You're the only one.

MRS. LINDEN. Yes?

NORA. I'm telling only you, do you understand? I saved Thorwald's life.

MRS. LINDEN. *(This startling statement leaving her completely unimpressed.)* Hm? Oh…

NORA. He would have died but for me.

MRS. LINDEN. I thought it was Italy that saved him.

NORA. Yes, but I…

MRS. LINDEN. *(A very practical person.)* Well, it was nice your father left you the money.

NORA. That's what Thorwald thinks…what everybody thinks. Papa didn't leave us a penny. I got the money myself.

MRS. LINDEN. You got it? All of it?

NORA. Every bit of it. Well, now what do you have to say?

> *(Now that she has got her friend astonished, she can rise and move away.)*

MRS. LINDEN. But, my dear, where did you find it? Did you win it in the lottery?

NORA. Lottery! Why any old fool could have done that!

MRS. LINDEN. But where else would you have managed to pick up so much? Naturally you couldn't borrow it.

NORA. *(Strolling around the two sofas, upstage, simply delighted with herself.)* No? And why not?

MRS. LINDEN. A wife, borrow money without her husband's consent?

NORA. I never said I borrowed it. Perhaps I got it some other way.

(*Conscious of herself, almost posing.*)

I may have got it from an admirer! After all, I'm not an altogether unattractive woman…

(*She reclines on the right-hand sofa, deliberately a picture.*)

MRS. LINDEN. (*Rises.*) Don't be ridiculous, Nora!

NORA. Just dying of curiosity, aren't you?

MRS. LINDEN. (*Coming over to the sofas, genuinely worried.*) Now look here, my dear, haven't you been a little reckless?

NORA. (*Now firmly on top of the situation.*) You mean reckless enough to save my husband's life?

MRS. LINDEN. (*Sitting on the left-hand sofa.*) Well, perhaps a little rash…without his consent to go and…

NORA. (**CHRISTINA** *is really being a little dense.*) Yes, and suppose it was fatal for him to know! Do you think he realized how ill he was? The doctors depended on me to do the worrying about that, and I did!

MRS. LINDEN. Why, Nora! How wonderful!

NORA. (*Moving over beside her.*) I used diplomacy, I tell you! (*Talleyrand couldn't have done better.*) I said I was just longing for a trip abroad, I cried and carried on and said he ought to think of my condition…

MRS. LINDEN. Good.

NORA. But when I barely hinted that he might just borrow the money…Ohhhh! You should have heard him!

MRS. LINDEN. His principles.

NORA. He made big speeches about his duty, how it was up to him to guide me and protect me from having such whims…and so he talked, and so I saved him.

MRS. LINDEN. Nora! But I should think your father would have told him the money didn't come from him.

NORA. (*She has an answer for this too.*) Oh he couldn't, because just then Papa died. So Thorwald, with all his grand ideas about independence, owes everything to me!

MRS. LINDEN. Haven't you ever told him?

NORA. Christina! What are you thinking of? Why, Thorwald thinks debts are immoral...almost criminal. If he ever found out what I'd done, our home just wouldn't be the same, that's all.

MRS. LINDEN. But won't you ever tell him?

NORA. Oh, after a great many years, perhaps...when I'm not so young.

> (*This is too much for* **CHRISTINA**'s *sense of humor.*)

Don't laugh, Christina. I mean when Thorwald isn't so much in love with me. When it isn't fun for him any longer to see me skipping about and dressing up and acting. Then it might be good to have something in reserve.

MRS. LINDEN. Oh, Nora, Nora!

NORA. Oh, but it's been so hard! Installments to meet, and interest, and interest on the installments... And all the time I had to pinch and plan...a little bit here, there, anywhere I could. I never could take any of the housekeeping money, because naturally Thorwald had to live well. And I couldn't let the children go about badly dressed...every penny I had for them I spent on them.

MRS. LINDEN. Poor Nora! So it had to come out of your own pocket money?

NORA. Yes, of course. I did the whole thing by myself! And besides that, I made money other ways. Just before Christmas last winter I was so lucky... I got a heap of copying to do. So every night I shut myself up and worked till long after midnight.

MRS. LINDEN. And how much have you been able to pay off?

NORA. Well, I can't say exactly. It's so hard to keep that sort of thing clear. I... I know that...well, that I paid off all I could scrape together anyway. Oh! Sometimes, Christina, I just didn't know which way to turn. Do you know what I used to think?

MRS. LINDEN. What?

NORA. That a nice rich man was in love with me.

MRS. LINDEN. What?

NORA. A nice one, who died right off. And so when they opened his will, they saw these words, in great big letters—"Pay over at once everything of which I die possessed to that charming creature, Mrs. Nora Helmer!"

MRS. LINDEN. But Nora, darling, what man are you talking about?

NORA. Oh, dear, can't you understand? There wasn't any man...it was just what I used to dream and dream when I was frantic for money. But it's all finished now. *(She rises, crosses center.)* I don't care anything about him or his will. My troubles are over. Oh, Christina, isn't it glorious to think of? Free from all those cares... absolutely free! Now I'll be able to play and have a good time with the children... I can get lots of things for the house, really good things, just what Thorwald will like. Oh, what a wonderful thing it is to be alive and to be happy!

> *(She crosses to Christina and embraces her ecstatically.*
>
> *The doorbell rings, and we see* **ELLEN** *come from the kitchen into the vestibule, to open it. Christina gets up.)*

MRS. LINDEN. Perhaps I'd better go...

NORA. No, no, stay! It's sure to be someone for Thorwald.

> *(***CHRISTINA** *walks left.* **NORA** *looks curiously out into the vestibule to see the visitor.* **ELLEN** *comes to the left-center doors.)*

ELLEN. If you please, ma'am, there's a gentleman to see Mr. Helmer.

NORA. Who is it?

> *(We see him only vaguely through the glass, but hear his voice, as he identifies himself.* **ELLEN** *closes the front door and returns to the kitchen.* **NORA** *becomes almost visibly on the alert.)*

KROGSTAD. It's I, Mrs. Helmer.

NORA. Oh! What is it? What do you want with my husband?

> *(***CHRISTINA***, way left, by the stove, hears the voice, and half turns, listening.)*

KROGSTAD. Just something to do with the bank... I have a little job there and I hear your husband is to be our new chief.

NORA. Oh, then it's not...?

KROGSTAD. Just a tiresome business matter, Mrs. Helmer... nothing more.

NORA. I'm afraid he's busy, but if you'll just knock on his door...

> *(He enters from the vestibule, knocks on* **HELMER**'s *door, and is bidden to enter. He doesn't notice* **CHRISTINA**, *but she has seen and heard him.* **NORA** *watches him go into the study. She has grown very, very thoughtful.)*

MRS. LINDEN. Nora...who was that man?

NORA. A Mr. Krogstad. Do you know him?

MRS. LINDEN. *(Starting to cross right, slowly; she, too, is thinking.)* I used to know him...years ago.

NORA. *(Beginning to cross to the stove.)* I understand his marriage wasn't happy.

MRS. LINDEN. *(Aware of the tense* **NORA** *has used.)* And he is a widower now?

NORA. Yes.

MRS. LINDEN. So...people do go on living after all. Is he in business with your husband? *(She sits on the right-hand sofa.)*

NORA. *(Stoking the fire with the poker.)* Oh, no, certainly not. There, now it'll burn up.

    (She hangs the poker on its hook, and comes center.)

I really don't know what he does. Anyway, the thing is to do something for you now...

    *(****HELMER****'s voice is heard as **DOCTOR RANK** opens the study door.)*

HELMER. *(From his study.)* My dear fellow, it's quite all right. You can stay...

DOCTOR RANK. No, no, don't bother, I'll just go have a talk with your wife...

    *(****DOCTOR RANK**** backs into the room, his coat over his arm, his hat and invariable stick in his hand. He turns and sees that **NORA** has a visitor.)*

Oh, I beg your pardon. I guess I'm just in the way wherever I go.

NORA. *(Coming up to take his things.)* No, no, come in, please! Doctor Rank, Mrs. Linden.

DOCTOR RANK. How do you do?

MRS. LINDEN. How do you do?

DOCTOR RANK. I believe I've heard your name before. I passed Mrs. Linden on the stairs as I came up.

    *(He walks slowly to the left-hand sofa, as **NORA**, placing his things on the piano bench, crosses behind him, and moves toward the study door.)*

MRS. LINDEN. I'm afraid I climb very slowly.

DOCTOR RANK. Oh, you're not very strong.

MRS. LINDEN. Well, just overworked.

    *(****DOCTOR RANK**** has sat down comfortably opposite **CHRISTINA**, on the other sofa. **NORA**, unnoticed, is listening at **HELMER**'s door.)*

DOCTOR RANK. Ah? So you've come up to the city to relax in a round of dissipation?

MRS. LINDEN. I've come to look for a job.

DOCTOR RANK. And is that an approved remedy for overwork?

MRS. LINDEN. One must live, Doctor Rank.

DOCTOR RANK. Yes, that seems to be the general opinion.

NORA. *(Who has kept one ear on their conversation.)* Oh come, Doctor Rank, you want to live yourself?

DOCTOR RANK. I seem to, don't I? Extraordinary, isn't it? No matter how miserable I feel, I still have a curious desire to hang on a little bit longer. And my patients, strangely enough, all seem to have the same mania. It's a disease... Even the fellow who just went in there seems infected with it.

MRS. LINDEN. Ah!

NORA. Whom do you mean?

DOCTOR RANK. That man Krogstad...you don't know him. Sly fellow, I hear. *(To* **CHRISTINA.***)* He was saying the same thing to Thorwald that you were just telling me.

NORA. *(Carefully dissembling her curiosity.)* What was he telling him?

DOCTOR RANK. He made the solemn announcement he must live. I was so overwhelmed that I departed.

NORA. What could he want with Thorwald?

DOCTOR RANK. Oh, I don't know. Something to do with the bank, apparently.

NORA. *(Remaining carefully behind him.)* The bank?

DOCTOR RANK. Yes, he works there. *(Quite idly said, turning to address* **CHRISTINA.***)* So there, you see, just another patient.

MRS. LINDEN. I'm afraid I don't follow you, Doctor.

DOCTOR RANK. I mean, he's alive, and he wants to stay that way.

MRS. LINDEN. *(Not sure whether she understands this mild cynicism.)* What then?

DOCTOR RANK. It's...delicate characters like that who seem to require the most elaborate treatment. There we have the thing that makes a hospital out of society.

(This apothegm has been listened to by both women: CHRISTINA with one personal interest, NORA with quite another. NORA, now to the left of DOCTOR RANK, suddenly laughs, spontaneous gaiety welling up in her.)

DOCTOR RANK. What are you laughing at? Do you have some ideas about society?

NORA. Oh, what do I care about your old society? I was laughing at something funny—terribly funny. *(She turns center and comes toward them.)* Are all the people who work at the bank dependent on Thorwald now?

DOCTOR RANK. H'mph! Do you call that funny?

NORA. *(Crossing airily behind him.)* Never mind, never mind. *(She is fumbling in the pocket of her skirt for her macaroons.)* But isn't it amusing that we...that Thorwald has such power over so many people? *(Suddenly she has the macaroons in her hand.)* Will you have a macaroon?

DOCTOR RANK. Dear, dear, macaroons! I thought they were contraband here.

NORA. Yes, but Christina brought me these.

MRS. LINDEN. Who, I?

NORA. *(Blandly covering her little lie.)* Oh, well! Don't be frightened. Thorwald's afraid they'll spoil my teeth. But, oh, bother, just for once! That's for you, Doctor Rank! *(She offers him one, which he takes.)* And this is for you, Christina! And as for me...*(Feeling all at once able to dare anything.)* I'll have one! Just a tiny one, or maybe two. *(She stops by the big chair, hardly able to contain her joy.)* Oh, dear! I am happy. There's only one thing in the world I really want.

(Unnoticed by any of them, KROGSTAD leaves HELMER's office by the door in the vestibule, crosses behind the glass panes, and goes out the front door.)

DOCTOR RANK. Yes? What is it?

NORA. Oh...something I wish I could say...in front of Thorwald.

DOCTOR RANK. Then why don't you say it?

NORA. It's so naughty.

MRS. LINDEN. Naughty?

DOCTOR RANK. Well, in that case you'd better not. But you might tell us. What is it you wish you could say in Thorwald's hearing?

NORA. (*Coming a little center, pleased with her own boldness.*) I want to say, "Hell and damnation!"

DOCTOR RANK. Ah! She's going to the dogs!

MRS. LINDEN. Good gracious me.

(*The door of* **HELMER**'s *study is opening.*)

DOCTOR RANK. Say it, here he comes.

NORA. Shhh! (*She hurries up to her husband.*) Darling, did you get rid of him?

HELMER. (*He has his portfolio under his arm and is full of business.*) Yes, he's just gone.

NORA. (*Seizing his arm before he can get away from her.*) Oh, Thorwald! This is Christina...she just came here all the way from—

HELMER. Christina? I'm afraid I don't...

NORA. Mrs. Linden, Thorwald... Christina Linden.

HELMER. (*Only politely.*) Ah...an old friend of my wife's, perhaps?

MRS. LINDEN. Yes. We used to go to school together.

NORA. Just imagine, darling! She came all this way just to have a word with you.

HELMER. Really?

(*He starts left, looking for some papers he's left around.*)

MRS. LINDEN. Well, not quite...

NORA. You see, Christina is awfully good at accounting...

(**NORA** *follows* **HELMER**, *who is preoccupied with his hunt for the documents.*)

Isn't that what it's called?... And naturally she wants

to work under a first-rate businessman to learn a lot more...

HELMER. *(Finding the papers on the piano, he carefully inserts them in his portfolio; he is still not much concerned about* **CHRISTINA**.*)* Very sensible.

NORA. So when she heard you were the new manager— it was telegraphed you know—she started right off... *(Carried along on the current of her own invention, she crosses past* **HELMER** *toward* **CHRISTINA**, *and is all but grooming her for the job.).*..and darling, you simply must do something for Christina, you absolutely must, Thorwald!

HELMER. *(On his way out, is beguilingly stopped.)* Well, it's not altogether impossible, of course. You're a widow, are you?

MRS. LINDEN. Yes.

HELMER. And you have had some experience in office work? *(Plainly giving her no encouragement.)*

MRS. LINDEN. A good deal.

HELMER. *(Going into the vestibule, to the coat tree, for his coat and hat.)* Well, there might just possibly be something...

NORA. See? What did I tell you?

HELMER. Perhaps you've come at a very opportune moment, Mrs. Linden.

> (**DOCTOR RANK** *rises to accompany* **HELMER** *on his way, and goes to the piano bench for his coat and hat.*)

MRS. LINDEN. How can I thank you?

HELMER. *(In the vestibule.)* Not at all.

> (**CHRISTINA** *gets up and hurries to the chair left of the piano for her coat.* **DOCTOR RANK** *crosses to the stove to warm his coat.*)

Well, I'll be back after a while.

DOCTOR RANK. Wait, I'm coming with you.

NORA. Don't be long, dear!

HELMER. Half an hour or so.

NORA. Are you going, too, Christina?

MRS. LINDEN. Yes, I must start hunting for lodgings.

(**NORA** *helps her friend with her coat.*)

HELMER. (*To* **CHRISTINA**.) Then I'll wait for you.

NORA. I'm so sorry we haven't a room to spare. Isn't it a pity?

MRS. LINDEN. I wouldn't think of troubling you. Thank you, Nora. (*She is in her coat and hat now, gathering up her gloves and bag.*) Good-bye, Nora, darling, and thank you for all your kindness.

(*They are both crossing toward the doors, right center.*)

NORA. Good-bye for a little while. Now listen, Christina, you'll come back this evening, won't you? (*Ushering* **CHRISTINA** *into the vestibule, she now turns back to* **DOCTOR RANK**.) And you, too, Doctor Rank, of course.

DOCTOR RANK. (*Lumbering across the stage in his overcoat.*) Yes, if I'm still alive.

NORA. Oh, you—what a way for a doctor to talk! Be careful, now, and wrap up tight.

(*The outer door opens, there is a shrill, little boy's whistle, and* **NORA**, *knowing her children are coming in from outdoors, rushes past everybody to meet them.*)

Oh! Here they are!... Oh, my darlings!... Mmmm-mmm..... .

(**EMMY** *runs into her mother's arms.* **IVAR**, *more dignified in the presence of adults, stands back. They are all in the vestibule.*)

NORA. Look, Christina, aren't they wonderful!

MRS. LINDEN. They're angels.

DOCTOR RANK. Brrr! What a draft! Let's not stand here chattering.

HELMER. Come, Mrs. Linden. Only mothers can stand such a temperature.

(The three go out the front door of the flat. NORA picks up EMMY and comes happily into the room with the child in her arms. IVAR follows more soberly behind, with ANNA, the nurse.)

EMMY. Mama, he threw a snowball and hit me!

IVAR. I did not!

EMMY. I hit him back.

NORA. Oh, my baby!… Mmm, such cheeks! Darling, you've been out hours! Aren't you frozen?

(She is in the big chair, taking off EMMY's little bonnet and coat.)

EMMY. I'm warm!

IVAR. I saw a dog, Mama.

(ANNA has helped him out of his coat, and he comes down to his mother.)

He ran after a man, and he growled.

EMMY. I saw the dog, too!

NORA. Did you, sweet?

IVAR. And the man picked up a stick, and the dog ran around biting people.

NORA. Really? I know he didn't bite you, did he, darling?

(IVAR, through with his story, sees the attractive packages on the table and skips up toward them.)

EMMY. I'd like a dog!

ANNA. I'll just take their coats, ma'am.

NORA. Oh, yes, Anna. And there's some hot coffee on the stove. Just go pour yourself some.

(ANNA goes into NORA's quarters, up left.)

EMMY. Can we play now, Mama?

NORA. Of course, darling. Any single thing you want! It's Christmas!

EMMY. I want to play Blind Man's Buff!

(IVAR, unobserved, is busily unwrapping one of

the packages.)

NORA. Blind Man's Buff! Oh, goody! *(She lifts **EMMY** up, sets her on her feet, kneels beside her.)* Now you know what you do first?

> *(**EMMY**, knowing very well, trots off into her mother's room.)*

IVAR. *(Who has now completely unwrapped a fine toy drum.)* This isn't for me, is it, Mama?

NORA. *(Almost childishly upset by this.)* Oh, Ivar, I didn't want you to see that until tomorrow!

IVAR. Well, I can wrap it up again!

EMMY. *(Toddling out of **NORA**'s room with **IVAR**'s scarf, which is to serve as a blindfold.)* Come on, Mama, let's play!

NORA. *(Taking the scarf and knotting it over her eyes.)* Run and hide, Emmy...in a good place! Turn me around, Ivar, then you hide!

> *(**EMMY** enthusiastically investigates the sofas as a place to hide, rejects them, and trots to the small side chair, down left. **IVAR** turns his mother around several times, and dodges under the piano. **NORA**, quite one of them by this time, blunders about, center stage, looking for them.)*

EMMY. *(In a whisper, from behind her chair.)* Look where I am, Ivar!

IVAR. *(Under the piano.)* Shhh!

EMMY. He's under the piano, Mama!

IVAR. *(Upset by his sister's treachery.)* Emmy!

> *(**KROGSTAD** appears in the right center doors, timid, hesitant, completely uncertain of himself, yet determined.)*

EMMY. *(Who sees him first.)* There's a man, Mama!

NORA. *(Still fumbling about blindfolded.)* What?

IVAR. It's a man!

> *(**IVAR** crawls out from under the piano, **EMMY** comes up to her mother.)*

KROGSTAD. *(Completely upset by this domestic scene.)* I'm sorry, I...

NORA. *(Pulling off the blindfold.)* Oh...what do you want?

KROGSTAD. You see, the door was open and I thought...I wanted to...

NORA. My husband's not at home, Mr. Krogstad...*(To her children, who are crowding around her.)* Go to Anna, dears.

KROGSTAD. I know that, but...

NORA. Then what did you come here for?

IVAR. Shall I stay here with you, Mama?

NORA. No, no, run along and see Anna!

EMMY. But I want to play!

NORA. *(Hurrying them out.)* Yes, we'll play in a minute...

EMMY. Is that a promise?

NORA. That's a real promise...*(She has them at her door.)* Take care of them, Anna.

> *(They exit, she shuts her door, and turns to face* **KROGSTAD.***)*

You wanted to see me?

KROGSTAD. It's just something...

NORA. But what for? It isn't the first of the month.

KROGSTAD. It isn't that. I wanted to ask you something. Can you spare a minute?

NORA. I suppose I can, but...

KROGSTAD. You see, I...when I was in the restaurant after I was here, I...

NORA. What's that?

KROGSTAD. I was sitting in the restaurant across the street and I saw your husband come out of here and...

NORA. I told you he wasn't home...

KROGSTAD. No, no...he went down the street with a lady.

NORA. Well?

KROGSTAD. Excuse me, but—would you mind telling me if it was a Mrs. Linden?

NORA. Why, yes!

KROGSTAD. I... I haven't seen her for so many years, and naturally I was surprised to see her coming out with your husband...

NORA. Oh, yes! She's going to be given a position at my husband's bank.

KROGSTAD. She is?!

NORA. Why, yes!

KROGSTAD. But...but now...?

NORA. Well, you see, sometimes a little influence with the right people, Mr. Krogstad...

KROGSTAD. You mean you had something to do with it?

NORA. Well, naturally, I did what I could for my friend.

KROGSTAD. Do you mean to tell me that Mrs. Linden is going to...?

NORA. Really, Mr. Krogstad, I'm not used to being questioned this way. You seem very much interested in Mrs. Linden.

KROGSTAD. Come, Mrs. Helmer, you know very well whose job it is your friend is getting.

NORA. What are you talking about?

KROGSTAD. *(Trying to assimilate this new blow.)* So I'm just to be thrown out, am I?

NORA. *(Honestly puzzled.)* What?

KROGSTAD. Oh, you needn't pretend you didn't know.

NORA. How dare you talk like that to me?

KROGSTAD. Oh, really! Look here, I can well understand why it wouldn't be pleasant for your dear friend to meet me. Influence, is it? Very well, Mrs. Helmer, then I must ask you to use your influence for me.

NORA. But I assure you I have...

KROGSTAD. There is still time for you to help me.

NORA. I have no influence whatever.

KROGSTAD. But you just said you had, Mrs. Helmer.

NORA. I meant nothing of the sort. I meant something quite different. Do you expect me to be able to tell my husband what to do?

KROGSTAD. I merely ask you...

NORA. *(Disturbed by his insistence, she moves away from him.)* I'm not afraid of you anymore. In a little while I'll be through with the whole business.

KROGSTAD. Please listen to me, Mrs. Helmer! *(He follows her, desperately needing to make his point.)* Try to understand that it is vital to me to keep my job in the bank!

NORA. I'm sorry, Mr. Krogstad...

KROGSTAD. I tell you I've got to keep it, that's all! I've got children and they're growing up. They need to have a father who's able to hold up his head in a respectable position... I tell you, I... There just aren't any jobs open to me, I've been cut off from everything!

NORA. Mr. Krogstad...

KROGSTAD. People just pass the word around quietly, don't you think I know? I tell you my job in the bank is the only chance I've got to get anywhere, and now your husband wants to kick me off the ladder and down into the mud again!

NORA. *(Trying to get even farther away from him.)* I'm sorry, Mr. Krogstad, but I just can't listen.

KROGSTAD. You've got to listen!

NORA. Mr. Krogstad, are you threatening me?

KROGSTAD. *(Miserably turning away from her.)* I don't care what you call it... I...

NORA. Mr. Krogstad, would you tell my husband I owe you money?

      *(**KROGSTAD** simply shrugs and turns away.)*

Why, you ought to be ashamed of yourself! When it's all my own secret and I'm so proud of it! Why, if he heard about it that way, there's no telling how unpleasant it would be!

KROGSTAD. Unpleasant!

NORA. Well, you just try it. It will be much worse for you, because then my husband will see what a bad man you are and you certainly won't keep your job!

KROGSTAD. Yes, it was very bad of me to lend you money when your husband was dying.

NORA. And if he does find out about it, why, then he'll pay you right off and we'll have nothing more to do with you.

KROGSTAD. Mrs. Helmer, I'm afraid there are some things you don't understand very well. Let me make them clearer for you.

NORA. You needn't bother.

KROGSTAD. When your husband was ill, you came to me to borrow a sum of money…a large sum of money. I promised to find it for you.

NORA. What's all that got to do with…

> *(She sits in the big chair, left, not wanting to listen.)*

KROGSTAD. I promised to find you the money under certain conditions. Do you remember what they were?

NORA. *(In a mood chiefly of exasperation.)* Ohhhh!

KROGSTAD. You probably didn't do much thinking about them because you were so busy taking care of your husband. Let me remind you what they were. I promised to find you the money in exchange for a written agreement which I drew up.

NORA. Well, I signed it, didn't I?

KROGSTAD. Yes. You did. And then I added a few lines, making your father sponsor for the amount. Your father was to sign this.

NORA. Was to? He did sign it!

KROGSTAD. Did he, Mrs. Helmer?

NORA. You know he did!

KROGSTAD. Do you remember I left the date blank? Your father was to date his signature himself.

NORA. Yes, and I…

KROGSTAD. Then I gave you the paper to send to your father. Isn't that right, Mrs. Helmer?

NORA. Yes.

KROGSTAD. And of course you did it at once.

NORA. Yes, of course!

KROGSTAD. And five or six days afterwards, Mrs. Helmer, you brought the paper back to me, with his signature, and I gave you the money.

NORA. Well, haven't I made my payments on time?

KROGSTAD. *(Moving on relentlessly to the next peg of his argument.)* Mrs. Helmer, your father was very ill, wasn't he?

NORA. He was on his death bed.

KROGSTAD. Tell me, Mrs. Helmer—do you happen to remember the day he died? The day of the month, I mean?

NORA. It was the twenty-ninth of September.

KROGSTAD. *(He has now the necessary admission in his hands.)* Ah! That's correct. But you see, I made a little investigation for myself, and I discovered a rather remarkable fact, which I can't quite explain…

> *(Surer of himself now, he turns away as if to exit.* **NORA** *rises and is after him.)*

NORA. What remarkable fact? What are you trying…

KROGSTAD. The remarkable fact is, or seems to be, that your father signed this paper three days after his death.

NORA. What? I don't understand—

KROGSTAD. Well, neither do I, Mrs. Helmer. Here your father dies on the twenty-ninth of September…*(He reaches into an inside pocket for his wallet, where he carries* **NORA***'s promissory note.)*…and here he signs his name on October the second. There's the date, don't you see? Now isn't that remarkable?

> *(Unconsciously,* **NORA** *reaches for the piece of paper, and* **KROGSTAD** *draws it back.* **NORA** *is utterly astonished that he should think her capable of snatching it or destroying it.)*

KROGSTAD. Perhaps you can explain it? The trouble seems to be that the words "October second" and the year, don't seem to be in your father's handwriting. They're in somebody else's. But that could be explained, too—possibly your father just forgot to date his signature and somebody else added the date hastily, without thinking very hard. Still, that's nothing to worry about. It's the signature that counts. It's genuine, Mrs. Helmer...isn't it?

> (**NORA** *has turned slowly away, stopping, quite quiet now, no longer protesting, behind the big chair.*)

Your father really did write his name here himself... didn't he?

NORA. *(After a pause.)* No. I wrote it.

KROGSTAD. Do you realize what you're admitting? That was a very dangerous thing to do, Mrs. Helmer.

NORA. *(Honestly not seeing that anything important is involved.)* Why? You'll have your last payment in a few days.

KROGSTAD. Do you mind if I ask you one more question? Why didn't you send this paper to your father?

NORA. How could I do such a thing? He was too ill to be worried about it.

KROGSTAD. Then don't you think it might have been better to give up your trip? After all...

NORA. *(Pursuing her own logic, out of her own integrity.)* But I couldn't possibly think of such a thing! It was to save my husband's life!

KROGSTAD. Well, but, Mrs. Helmer you were deceiving me.

NORA. Oh, for Heaven's sake, suppose I was!

KROGSTAD. Mrs. Helmer, you really don't seem to understand what you've done! Mrs. Helmer...do you know, I did something just about like that once, and it ruined me?

NORA. How could it?

KROGSTAD. It wasn't a bit worse or a bit more important than what you've just confessed to me.

NORA. You mean you took a risk to save someone's life?

KROGSTAD. The law, Mrs. Helmer, takes no account of motives.

NORA. *(For the first time in her life understanding this, and making up her own mind about it.)* Then the law must be very bad.

KROGSTAD. *(Crossing toward the vestibule.)* Bad or not, if I take this paper to court, the law will condemn you exactly as it did me.

NORA. I don't believe it! As if I didn't have the right to save my father from worry when he was dying! As if anyone should tell me that I hadn't the right to save my husband's life! I don't know very much about law, and I don't want to, if that's the way it is. But I'm certain they'd let you do that. Why, the idea of not knowing they would, when you're a lawyer! You must be a very poor one.

KROGSTAD. Maybe I am. But I do understand something about this business you and I are in together. And now you can do exactly as you please… *(He picks up his hat off the table.)* But let me tell you one thing…if I'm thrown off into the mud again, there'll be others to keep me company.

> *(He goes into the vestibule and out the front door, leaving* **NORA** *alone with the obvious and ominous import of his visit. She is alone for only a moment before her children come bursting into the room.* **EMMY** *has been made ready for bed, and is in a white flannel nightdress and pink slippers.)*

EMMY. Mama, can we come in?

IVAR. Can we go on playing now, Mama?

EMMY. *(Tugging at her.)* Come on, Mama!

NORA. *(Kneeling down beside them, to hold their complete attention.)* Listen to what Mama says. Don't you ever tell anybody there was a man here. Cross your heart. Do you hear?

EMMY. Why?

NORA. You mustn't even tell Papa.

EMMY. *(As* **IVAR** *walks away; considering this proposition.)* Why?

NORA. Because you mustn't, darling.

IVAR. We won't say anything. Hear, Emmy?

> *(He puts a finger to his lips, a gesture* **EMMY** *faithfully duplicates.)*

Now will you play?

NORA. *(Rises, turns away.)* No, no, not now. I can't.

EMMY. Won't you come in and even read to us?

IVAR. You promised you'd play just as soon as he went!

NORA. Shhh! Go on back to Anna, please, my darlings...

EMMY. *(Pretty discouraged.)* Oh, dear, oh, dear...

NORA. Emmy, do you hear me? Anna, take care of them and see that they don't...

> *(The children exit.* **NORA** *closes her door, then moves slowly back into the room.* **ELLEN** *comes from the kitchen with the Christmas tree, ready for trimming, and sets it on the table between the sofas.)*

ELLEN. Well, Mrs. Helmer, here it is!

NORA. Oh...

ELLEN. There now, doesn't it smell good? Shall I help you?

NORA. No, no, thank you, Ellen.

ELLEN. It makes such a picture. *(She returns to the kitchen.)*

> *(***NORA***, her mind anywhere but on Christmas preparations now, sits on the piano bench a moment. She makes an effort to throw off the burden of her thought, rises, picks up a small wicker basket of Christmas tree trimmings, comes down to the tree, opens the basket, and fastens a single hanging to the tree. She picks up another and is reaching up to tie it on the branches when she hears the street door to the house slam, below. The bit of trimming drops from her hand and breaks. She looks toward the vestibule and her own house door, expecting anything.* **HELMER** *enters the*

vestibule and, passing the coat tree, comes to the glass doors to the living room, hat and coat on, the inevitable portfolio under his arm.)

NORA. Oh, Thorwald! Back already?

HELMER. *(Elaborately casual.)* Has anybody been here?

NORA. *(With the thorough naïveté of the good liar.)* Here? No.

HELMER. *(Retreats to the coat tree to dispose of his hat and coat.)* That's strange. *(Enters the room and crosses soberly behind her, to the piano bench, where he puts down his portfolio.)* I saw Krogstad leave the house.

NORA. *(Busily trimming the tree now.)* Krogstad? Well, he really was here for just a minute.

HELMER. *(Turning.)* Nora!

NORA. What? I tell you it was just for a minute!

HELMER. Nora, look at me. I'm very, very much surprised. Krogstad has been asking you to put in a good word for him, hasn't he? Hmm?

NORA. *(She crosses to him, prettily.)* Are you going to be angry with me?

HELMER. And you were supposed to do it just as if you'd thought of it yourself. Isn't that right? Without ever mentioning the fact that he came here and put you up to it?

NORA. Yes...but I...

HELMER. No, Nora! And you could stoop to that! To speak to such a man, to make him a promise! And then to tell a lie about it...to me!

NORA. A lie?

HELMER. Didn't you say nobody had been here? That's lying. You won't do that again, will you?

(She doesn't answer. He takes her chin in his hand and turns her face to his.)

Will you?

(This promise exacted, he turns away, picks up his portfolio and walks to his big chair, left.)

Well, we won't say any more about it. *(He selects a cigar*

from his pocket case, settles back in the chair comfortably.)
Mmm! That chair feels good.

(He lights his cigar, takes his glasses from their case, puts them on, opens his portfolio, and proceeds, businesslike, to get to work.)

NORA. *(Going on with her trimming, her mind plainly somewhere else.)* Thorwald...

(He barely mumbles an acknowledgment.)

We have to get ready for the Stenborg's fancy dress ball the day after tomorrow. *(She takes a tentative step or two toward him.)* Are you very busy, Thorwald?

HELMER. *(Without looking up.)* Mm...mm.

NORA. *(Closer to him now.)* What are all those papers?

HELMER. *(Only vaguely listening.)* Bank business.

NORA. Already?

HELMER. What? Oh, just a few changes in the staff. It won't take me very long.

NORA. *(Leaning over from behind his chair.)* Darling, I wish you weren't busy. Do you know why? Because if you weren't I'd ask you a big, big, big favor!

HELMER. Hm?

NORA. You have such wonderful taste, darling, I...well, you know I don't value anybody's opinion in the whole world the way I do yours! So I want to make a big impression at the ball, and I wondered if you would tell me what I'm going to be, help me with my costume...

HELMER. *(Scarcely hearing her.)* What? Why, yes...certainly, certainly.

NORA. Please, darling, I just can't manage without you!

HELMER. Well, we'll see what we can do.

NORA. *(Pleased out of all proportion to the size of the favor he grants.)* Oh, Thorwald, you're such an angel! *(She whirls up to her roses, moves them to a slightly better place on the piano.)* These roses look wonderful, don't they? *(All in the same breath she returns right, to the tree, slipping easily into* *the subject really on her mind.)* Tell me, was it something really awful this Krogstad got into trouble over?

HELMER. *(Completely engrossed in his papers.)* Forgery, that's all. You know what that means.

NORA. But...don't you think he might have been forced to do it?

HELMER. Perhaps. *(Pause.)* I'm not so hard-hearted as to condemn a man for a single slip.

NORA. No, of course not, Thorwald.

HELMER. A man can redeem his character if he admits his crime and takes his punishment.

NORA. Crime?

HELMER. *(All this is said idly, into his papers, and NORA receives thus her own indictment alone, with no sense of communication with him.)* But Krogstad didn't. He dodged, and used all kinds of tricks. He was disbarred, of course, but he should have been sent to jail. It's really too bad to see how the affair corrupted his character.

NORA. But...don't you think?... He had responsibilities, children. After all, he might have done it for their sakes.

HELMER. That's the worst of it. It's like a poison, especially for the children.

NORA. How do you mean?

HELMER. Because they're the most impressionable. He has to lie and sham, with that ugly thing on his conscience. It poisons the entire atmosphere around him.

NORA. *(Unable now to go on with even a pretense of trimming the tree, she drifts up to the piano bench, and sits.)* Thorwald... do you mean that?

HELMER. I've seen it time and time again. It's really amazing to see how criminal tendencies in children can be traced to lying parents. Yes, I suppose this Krogstad has been contaminating his poor children for years.

NORA. But how?

HELMER. By his life of lies and deceit, of course...they're all drawn into it with him. Sad, isn't it? I can sympathize with you when you feel sorry for him. But you'll promise not to say any more about it, hm?

(Without even being aware of just what part of the room she's in, he extends his right hand toward her. Nothing happening, he looks around, surprised.)

Why, what's this? Aren't we going to shake hands on it?

(Mechanically responding to the little ritual, she gets up and comes toward him, putting her left hand in his right.)

There, it's a bargain.

*(**NORA** moves a step away.)*

Oh, I'm worn out. I don't mind telling you I would have found it impossible to work with him. It makes me feel sick to come in contact with that kind of man.

*(**NORA**, as if stifled, takes a deep breath.)*

NORA. It's so hot here!

(She moves slowly to the right-hand sofa and sits.)

HELMER. Yes, it is rather close. *(He methodically folds up his portfolio, rises, strolls toward his study door.)* I'd better finish with these papers before dinner.

(Caught by some music left open on the piano, he pauses, kneels on the bench, and plays a few bars, breaking off in the middle of a phrase. He leaves the piano and walks to his door and opens it.)

I think I may have an idea for your costume tonight.

*(He leaves her alone, **NORA** staring forward. After the merest of pauses, **ANNA** opens her door and comes into the room.)*

ANNA. The children are just begging to come in, Miss Nora.

NORA. What?

ANNA. The children...will you have them in here?

NORA. No, no...not now, Anna.

*(**ANNA**, obediently and uncomprehendingly, turns*

and goes out, closing **NORA**'s *door after her.)*

(The curtain slowly falls.)

ACT TWO

(*The same room, Christmas Day, in the late afternoon. The tree has been stripped of its presents; the candles, lit the night before for the children, have been burnt low and snuffed out. The tree has been moved to the table in the upstage right corner. The door to* **HELMER**'s *study is open, the door to* **NORA**'s *room and nursery is closed.*)

(**NORA** *sits in the big chair, left, alone, thoughtful, staring ahead of her.*)

(*The door to her room opens and* **ANNA** *comes in with* **NORA**'s *tarantella costume, folded neatly in a box.*)

ANNA. (*Crossing to the table by the sofas.*) Look! Miss Nora, I've found it.

NORA. Anna, you frightened me. What is it?

ANNA. The fancy dress for the party. I'm afraid it needs mending.

NORA. I wish I could tear it into a hundred thousand pieces!

ANNA. No, no…you'll see, it just needs a little patience—a few stitches here and there.

NORA. Well, I'll ask Mrs. Linden to help me. (*She rises.*) Yes, I think I'll go now.

ANNA. In weather like this! Oh, no, Miss Nora, you'll catch cold, you'll be ill.

NORA. (*Crossing past her, she looks listlessly at the costume.*) There are worse things than to be ill, Anna. What are the children doing?

ANNA. Well, they're playing with their presents, poor little things.

45

NORA. Have they been…do they ask for me?

ANNA. Well, of course they're so used to having their mama playing with them.

NORA. Yes, I know, but you can see, Anna, that we can't go on…

> (*Below, on the ground floor, the front door slams. The sound is disturbing to* **NORA**, *to whom it may mean anything. She moves to the vestibule doors and opens them a bit. Thoughtfully, she listens. There is no bell at her own door, so she closes the vestibule doors, and moves to the table.*)

I mean, it's best we change all that a little.

ANNA. (*Not seeing at all.*) Yes, I see.

NORA. In the future, I shan't be with them quite so much.

ANNA. That's as you think best, of course…still, little children get used to anything.

NORA. Yes, they do, don't they? I suppose…do you think, that children can ever come to forget their mother… I mean, if…

ANNA. Gracious me, forget their mother?…

NORA. Tell me, Anna… I've often wondered about it—how you were able to give your child over to strangers like that? I mean, just give it away, entirely?

ANNA. Oh, that was when I had to come and nurse my little Nora.

NORA. (*Turning a little toward her.*) Yes, but Anna, how could you do it?

ANNA. When I had the chance of such a good place? When you come to think of it, it was very lucky for a girl in my position to find something at that time.

NORA. Yes, but your daughter…didn't she forget you?

ANNA. Oh, no, miss, no. She wrote to me, you know, when she was confirmed; and she wrote to me again when she was married. Yes.

NORA. (*Coming to her, putting her arms around her, burying her head in* **ANNA**'s *breast.*) Dear, dear Anna, you were a very good mother to me when I was little.

ANNA. My poor little dear…she had nobody else but me.

NORA. And if ever my children should need anybody like that, I'm sure you'd be just as…*(She turns away)* Oh, that's so silly! Go in to the children, Anna.

(**ANNA** *obediently starts left.*)

What a state this is!

ANNA. *(On her way out.)* Now, now, I know my little one will be the prettiest at the ball tomorrow night—just a little patience, my dear, just a little patience.

(*She exits, closing* **NORA**'*s door behind her.* **NORA** *drifts toward the piano bench, plainly trying to master the current of her thought.*)

NORA. To forget! To forget! To forget! *(Eyeing her coat, muff and gloves, which have been laid ready on the bench. She picks up the gloves.)* My gloves—my lovely, lovely gloves…*(She sits down on the bench, pressing the warm muff to her face.)* And my muff, my beautiful, beautiful muff.

(*Out in the vestibule, the doorbell rings.* **ELLEN** *appears from the kitchen, opens the door, letting in* **CHRISTINA**. **NORA** *gets up and opens the vestibule doors.*)

Oh, it's you, Christina!

MRS. LINDEN. *(Removing her hat, by the coat tree.)* Yes—why? What's the matter?

NORA. *(Staring into the vestibule, toward the door.)* Wasn't there anybody else there?

MRS. LINDEN. *(Taking off her coat.)* No, of course not.

NORA. *(Going into the vestibule to embrace her friend.)* Oh, I'm so glad you've come, Christina!

MRS. LINDEN. They told me you'd called at my house.

NORA. *(Coming into the living room while* **CHRISTINA**, *in the vestibule, gives a final pat to her hair.)* I was just passing by. You see, there's something you must help me with.

MRS. LINDEN. *(Entering the living room.)* Yes, Nora, of course.

NORA. *(Sitting on the sofa, indicating the seat beside her.)* Let's sit here on the sofa. There, Christina. I'm so glad you're here—I'm terribly, terribly upset. You see, tomorrow night there's a fancy dress ball at Consul Stonberg's apartment upstairs...

> *(**CHRISTINA** smiles a little at a case of nerves developed over so tiny a cause, and **NORA** is forced to smile, too.)*

Thorwald wants me to go as one of these Neapolitan fisher girls, and he wants me to dance the tarantella, you know, that's their native dance—I learned it at Capri.

MRS. LINDEN. I see.

NORA. Yes, that's what Thorwald wants. And this is the thing... I mean. Look at this costume! *(She half lifts it from the box.)* It's all so torn and in pieces, I don't know what to...

MRS. LINDEN. *(Taking the dress from her.)* Darling, what a child you are. There's nothing really the matter with it—just some of the trimming's come loose here and there.

> *(She looks about her, sees a set of spools, the sewing equipment of the house, under a glass dome on the side table, down right, rises and goes to it.)*

All we want's a needle and thread...*(Lifts off the glass dome, selecting a needle from the collection.)* Ah, here we are!

NORA. Oh, Christina, how kind you are!

MRS. LINDEN. *(Slipping a thimble on her finger.)* There... So you'll be all dressed up in costume tomorrow night. I do want to see you in it. I'll stop in for just a minute and look at you.

> *(She sits down with the dress, on the sofa opposite **NORA**, and starts efficiently to do the small mending required.)*

There. You know, I forgot to thank you for the pleasant evening last night.

NORA. Last night? Oh, that didn't seem so pleasant as usual. You should have come earlier, Christina. Thorwald can always make it so bright. He really has a gift that way.

(**NORA** *has risen, and moved absently across the room, toward the left window.*)

MRS. LINDEN. So have you. When it comes to that, you're your own father's daughter. But tell me, Nora, is Doctor Rank always as gloomy as he was last night?

NORA. No. Last night, he was really quite bad. You see, he has a dreadful illness, poor Doctor Rank. (*Drifting toward the center, and back down left.*) They say…his father was a horrible man, who kept mistresses…and all sorts of things, and so his son has been ill all his life—as a result of it, you understand.

MRS. LINDEN. Why, my darling Nora! How on earth do you come to know about such things as that?

NORA. Oh, when one's had two children, one learns a few things. One gets to meet nurses, and they talk of this and that—you know.

MRS. LINDEN. (*Sticking to her subject, as* **NORA** *wanders vaguely about the room, her mind very much elsewhere.*) Tell me something. Does Doctor Rank come here every day?

NORA. Every day of his life. Why, Doctor Rank's like one of the family.

MRS. LINDEN. But, listen, Nora—is he quite sincere? I mean, he seems to me to be rather given to flattering people.

NORA. Why, no, just the opposite, Christina. What made you think so?

MRS. LINDEN. When you introduced us yesterday, he said that he'd often heard my name. But I noticed that afterwards, when your husband came in, he had no notion of who I was at all. Now, how could Doctor Rank…?

NORA. Oh…well you see, it's this way. Thorwald…loves me so that, well, as he says himself, he wants me all to himself. When we were first married, really! He was almost jealous whenever I mentioned any of my old friends. And, naturally, I just gave up talking about them.

> (*She walks left, toward the stove, and stops a moment to warm her hands.*)

NORA. But with Doctor Rank, I often talk over all the old times; oh, all sorts of little things, and people I remember; he likes to hear about them.

MRS. LINDEN. Listen, Nora—in many ways you're still a child. I'm older than you, and I've had so much more experience, of all kinds. Let me tell you something— you ought to get clear of all this with Doctor Rank.

NORA. (*Just not understanding.*) Get clear, Christina? Clear of what?

MRS. LINDEN. The whole thing, the whole affair. That's what I should say.

NORA. (*Coming right, toward her.*) What affair?

MRS. LINDEN. Don't you remember, you were talking yesterday about a rich admirer, who was to find you some money, so that you...

NORA. (*Approaching the sofa.*) Yes, an admirer that never existed, worse luck. Yes, what about it?

MRS. LINDEN. Has Doctor Rank money?

NORA. Yes, I suppose so.

MRS. LINDEN. And nobody to provide for?

NORA. Nobody...but...?

MRS. LINDEN. And he comes here every day?

NORA. Certainly. I told you...

MRS. LINDEN. I should really think he'd have better taste.

NORA. (*Absolutely astonished.*) Christina! I don't understand what you're talking about.

MRS. LINDEN. Nora, don't pretend. Do you think I can't guess who lent you all that money for Thorwald's illness?

NORA. Christina! Have you lost your mind! How could you ever imagine such a thing?

MRS. LINDEN. *(Surprised in her turn.)* Then it wasn't he?

NORA. Oh, no. No, of course not. It never occurred to me for a minute...besides, at that time he didn't have any money to lend. He came into some property later.

MRS. LINDEN. Oh, I see. Well, anyway, I think that was a lucky thing for you, Nora.

NORA. *(With a part of her mind considering the idea, for the first time.)* The thought never would have occurred to me to ask Doctor Rank. But if I had, Christina, I'm perfectly certain...

MRS. LINDEN. Yes, but of course you wouldn't have; I mean...behind your husband's back.

NORA. After all, the other thing's behind my husband's back, too. Yes, and that I must get clear of, as you call it, and as soon as possible!

MRS. LINDEN. *(To **NORA** as she walks away from her.)* I should think so.

NORA. *(Turning back to her.)* A man can manage things like that so much better than a woman.

MRS. LINDEN. Especially one's own husband.

NORA. Any man. When you've paid up all the money, Christina, you get the paper back, isn't that so?

MRS. LINDEN. Of course.

NORA. *(Moving away again, her mood almost febrile.)* And then I can tear it into a hundred thousand pieces, the nasty, horrid thing, and burn it up!

MRS. LINDEN. Nora—you're hiding something from me!

NORA. *(Turning toward her, startled.)* Why? Does it show in my face?

MRS. LINDEN. Something has happened since yesterday. Nora! Nora, what is it? *(She rises.)* Let me try and help you!

NORA. *(Not yet ready to unburden her heart to **CHRISTINA**.)* Oh, Christina, it's...

(The street door slams below.)

NORA. Oh, that must be Thorwald. Do you mind, Christina? Thorwald simply hates the sight of any sewing or dress-making going on…

> *(She is hurrying* **CHRISTINA**, *with the tarantella costume, toward her door up left, as* **HELMER** *comes into the vestibule, and is removing his hat and coat.)*

Do you mind just going into the nursery? Anna's there and she'll help you.

MRS. LINDEN. Very well. But, Nora, I shan't leave the house until you tell me all about it!

> *(She goes out, up left, leaving the door ajar.* **NORA** *crosses to greet* **HELMER**, *who comes into the living room, his portfolio under his arm.)*

NORA. Oh, Thorwald, I just couldn't wait for you to come home!

HELMER. *(Giving her a husbandly kiss.)* Who was that? The dressmaker?

NORA. No, just Christina. She's helping me with my costume. Oh, darling, it's going to be simply beautiful!

HELMER. *(Walking over to the stove to warm his hands.)* It was a very good idea of mine, hm?

NORA. Oh, wonderful! But it was good of me, too.

HELMER. Good of you?

NORA. I mean, giving in to you about dancing the tarantella.

HELMER. *(Turning away from the stove.)* Aren't you supposed to give in to your husband? Really, dear, you're such a giddy…Well, I won't disturb you now. *(Starting for his study.)* I suppose you're in the middle of fitting and "trying on."

> *(Goes into his study, puts the portfolio on his desk.)*

NORA. *(Drifting to the piano bench.)* Going in to work?

HELMER. Yes, I've just come from the bank.

NORA. *(Sitting on the bench.)* Thorwald...

HELMER. Yes?

NORA. If the creature were to ask you for something, to beg you for something, very prettily...would you do it?

HELMER. That depends on what it is.

NORA. Now, listen, Thorwald, if only you'd be extra nice and kind...

HELMER. Nora, you can't mean what you were hinting at this morning?

NORA. Yes, Thorwald! I beg you, I implore you!

HELMER. *(Leaving his desk, coming into the doorway.)* Are you going to begin that again?

NORA. *(Rising, coming toward him.)* Yes, for my sake. Thorwald, you must let Krogstad keep his place in the bank.

HELMER. My dear Nora, it's his place I'm giving to your friend, Mrs. Linden.

NORA. *(Close to him now.)* Yes, darling, and that's so good of you. But instead of Krogstad, couldn't you just dismiss some other clerk?

HELMER. *(Getting seriously annoyed.)* Dismiss some other clerk? What's the matter with you, Nora? Just because you were impulsive enough to promise to put in a good word for him, I am to—

NORA. No, it's not that. It's not that I said anything to him. It's for your own sake, Thorwald! He can do so much harm...by talking and everything. I'm so terribly afraid of him.

HELMER. *(Coming closer a few steps.)* Oh, I see what's frightened you.

NORA. What do you mean?

HELMER. You're thinking of your father!

NORA. Yes, that's it, Thorwald! All those wicked things, those slanders people used to say about Papa.

HELMER. But, Nora, my child—between your father and me there's all the difference in the world! There were some grounds for them to talk about your father. With me, on the other hand, there are none, and I hope—

NORA. Yes, but I hear he's rather malicious and there's no telling what…*(Cozily taking his arm.)* Thorwald, we want to live here, quietly and happily—you and I and the children, don't we, Thorwald? That's why I beg you and implore you…

HELMER. Yes. And the more you plead for him, the more you make it impossible for me to keep him on. My child, everyone at the bank knows that I'm getting rid of him. If it got 'round now that the new president has changed his mind because his wife could twist him 'round her little finger—

NORA. Thorwald!

HELMER. —that would be talk enough! I'd be the laughingstock of the whole staff! People would say I was open to all kinds of outside influence—that I didn't have a mind of my own!

> *(In his anger he has walked away from her to behind the sofas. Now, a little reluctantly, he turns back to face her.)*

Besides, there's something that makes it absolutely out of the question for me to have Krogstad in the bank.

NORA. What?

HELMER. Well, at a pinch I could overlook the shady affair he was involved in a few years ago—

NORA. Oh, yes, Thorwald, I know you could!

HELMER. And I hear he's not bad at his job. But—I may as well confess it to you right off. He insists on calling me by my first name; the fact that we went to school together seems to give him the right. One of those boyish friendships you make before you've developed any judgment, and regret for the rest of your life. Yes, and he does it before other people! That's what makes it so awkward. It's always Thorwald this, and Thorwald that! I tell you it makes things absolutely intolerable… *(Moving toward his study.)* And I won't stand for it!

NORA. Why, Thorwald, you're not serious?

HELMER. *(Stops, turns back.)* No? Why not?

NORA. But a petty little thing like that?

HELMER. *(Comes slowly down center to her.)* Petty? You consider me petty?

NORA. No, Thorwald, no, on the contrary. That's why I'm so surprised.

HELMER. *(At his most severe now, as his pride has been touched.)* Never mind. So you think it's small of me to be affected by a thing like that. Very well. *(He strides to the vestibule doors. Yelling off.)* Ellen! *(He hurries into his study.)* We'll put an end to this once and for all.

NORA. What are you going to do?

> (**ELLEN** *comes from the kitchen to the vestibule doors.)*

HELMER. *(Coming out of the study, a letter on bank stationery in his hand.)* I want to settle this matter immediately. Here, Ellen, take this letter. The address is on it. It's just 'round the corner.

ELLEN. *(Takes it and exits to the kitchen.)* Yes, sir.

> (**HELMER**, *with no further look at* **NORA**, *heads back into the study.* **NORA** *runs up to him.)*

NORA. Thorwald! What was in that letter?

HELMER. *(Turning to face her.)* Krogstad's dismissal.

NORA. *(Clinging to him, with a desperation which baffles him.)* Call it back again, Thorwald! There's still time! For my sake, for your own! Listen, please, Thorwald, you don't know what might happen because of it!

HELMER. Now come, Nora, I suppose I can overlook this anxiety of yours, though I must say it's not very flattering to me. What do you expect me to do? Worry about being slandered or blackmailed by a wretched fellow like Krogstad? Really, I can forgive you only because I know it's proof of your love for me. And that's as it should be. Yes—yes, let what will happen; when it comes to the pinch I think you'll find my shoulders are broad enough to bear the burden.

NORA. Thorwald, what are you talking about?

HELMER. The whole burden…every bit of it.

NORA. *(Understanding something quite other than he intends.)* No, never, never. That you shall never…

> *(**NORA** moves to the table between the sofas. **HELMER** follows her.)*

HELMER. There, there. We'll do it together, then. We'll share it—man and wife. How would you like that? *(Takes her chin in his hands)* How frightened you look. Come, darling, stop worrying; it's just your imagination. Take my word for it. I'll tell you what! *(He picks up the tambourine out of the box, on the right table)* Take your tambourine and practice your tarantella. I'll close both doors to my study—you can make as much noise as you like!

> *(There is a special, distinctive ring at the doorbell.)*

That must be Rank. Keep him for a bit, will you, dear? I've got to go over some of these letters.

> *(He goes to his study, closing the doors. Knowing **ELLEN** is out on her errand to **KROGSTAD**, **NORA** crosses into the vestibule, to admit **DOCTOR RANK**.)*

NORA. *(Opening the front door.)* Good afternoon, Doctor Rank.

DOCTOR RANK. Good afternoon.

NORA. *(Coming back into the living room as **DOCTOR RANK** leaves his hat and coat on the coat tree.)* I knew you by your ring. Thorwald's not quite ready for you; he's busy over some papers he brought back from the bank.

DOCTOR RANK. *(Entering the room.)* And you?

> *(She has paused for a moment at the left side of the piano to glance at her hair in the mirror.)*

NORA. Oh, I'm very busy, too, but I always have time for you.

DOCTOR RANK. *(Crossing to the stove.)* Thank you; and I'm always ready to take advantage of that fact, as long as I can.

NORA. As long as you can? What does that mean?

DOCTOR RANK. *(Turning to her.)* Does that frighten you?

NORA. I think it's an odd expression. Isn't it? Do you expect anything to happen? *(Moving toward him a step.)*

DOCTOR RANK. Oh—something that's no surprise. I'll admit I didn't think it would come so soon, but…

NORA. Doctor Rank! Is there something you've really discovered?

    (He smiles faintly.)

No, no, tell me! Oh—you've discovered something about yourself.

DOCTOR RANK. Who else should it be?

NORA. *(Moving right, toward the sofas, a little.)* Doctor Rank…

DOCTOR RANK. *(Coming a little toward her.)* Yes. I've been auditing my life account—and it looks as if I'm bankrupt. Before very long, my poor carcass will be rotting in the churchyard.

NORA. Doctor Rank! What a dreadful way to talk!

DOCTOR RANK. Dreadful? Well, it's a dreadful business, and preceded by some dreadful preliminaries. There's one final test to be made, and then we'll know exactly when disintegration sets in. *(He crosses down right, passing her, toward the right-hand sofa.)* Ah, yes, there's something I want to tell you first. You know how Helmer shrinks from anything morbid; he must be spared all this—so keep him out of my sickroom.

NORA. Doctor Rank!…

DOCTOR RANK. Remember…I shall lock my door against him. *(He sits on the sofa.)* As soon as I'm certain of the worst, I shall send you my visiting card, and then you'll know that really serious things have begun.

NORA. *(Walking away.)* Oh, dear, you're in such a gloomy, bad humor today.

DOCTOR RANK. Yes, think of it! And my bad humor's all the worse, because I have to suffer from someone else's very good humor.

NORA. *(Coming back toward him.)* I won't listen! You know you're exaggerating. You just like to talk this way. Now, tonight you must be cheerful.

DOCTOR RANK. *(Responding playfully to her mood.)* Well, after all—the whole thing deserves to be laughed at. My poor spine has to suffer for my father's gay...dinners.

NORA. All that pâté de foie gras! And asparagus!

DOCTOR RANK. Yes, and truffles, too.

NORA. *(Sitting on the other sofa.)* Yes...truffles. And oysters... and champagne.

DOCTOR RANK. Oh, a great deal of champagne. And port.

NORA. What a pity that all those good things have to go to the spine.

DOCTOR RANK. Yes, and a spine that never had any good of them either.

NORA. Yes, indeed. That's the worst of it.

DOCTOR RANK. *(Quietly appreciating her humorous skating over the subject.)* Hm...

NORA. Why are you smiling?

DOCTOR RANK. No, it was you who were smiling.

NORA. Well, you smiled first.

DOCTOR RANK. You're deeper than I thought.

NORA. *(Rises on some strange current of energy and walks left.)* Oh, I'm in such a queer mood today. I'm just a little crazy today.

DOCTOR RANK. So I see.

NORA. *(Coming back toward him.)* Dear, dear Doctor Rank. Listen, you mustn't think of dying and leaving Thorwald and me.

DOCTOR RANK. Oh, you'll get over it beautifully. The absent are soon forgotten.

NORA. Do you think so?

DOCTOR RANK. *(Banteringly conscious of the absurdity of what he is saying.)* People make fresh ties...

NORA. Who makes fresh ties?

DOCTOR RANK. You and Thorwald will, when I'm gone. In fact, I think you're all rushing things a bit, aren't you? What was that Mrs. Linden doing here yesterday?

NORA. Oh! Surely you're not jealous of poor Christina?

DOCTOR RANK. *(Wholly playful.)* Yes, certainly I am. She will take my place here. Once I'm gone, this woman will perhaps—

NORA. Shhh! She's in there now!

> *(She points toward her room, and runs up to it, to close the partially open door.)*

DOCTOR RANK. *(Rising.)* Today, too...you see?

NORA. *(Running back to him.)* Only to mend my costume! Dear me, how unreasonable you are. Now do be good, Doctor Rank; put all these thoughts out of your head. Tomorrow night you'll see how beautifully I'm going to dance! You may think to yourself that I'm doing it all just to please you...and Thorwald, too, of course.
(She seats him on the right-hand sofa) Sit down here, Doctor Rank... I want to tell you something...

> *(But she can't quite bring herself to do it yet, so she goes to the box, on the table between the sofas, which contained her costume.)*

Oh, yes, and I want to show you something, too.

DOCTOR RANK. What is it?

NORA. *(Taking out a pair of shell-pink stockings, carefully ironed and folded, which she is to wear with the costume.)* Look!

DOCTOR RANK. *(Takes them in his hand.)* Silk stockings...

NORA. Flesh-colored. Aren't they beautiful? It's too dark in here now, but...*(As he slowly unfolds them.)* No, no, you must only look at the feet. Oh, well, I suppose you may look at the rest, too.

DOCTOR RANK. *(He has never been in such intimate touch with her before.)* Hm...

NORA. What are you looking so thoughtful about? You don't think they'll fit me?

DOCTOR RANK. *(As she takes the stockings from him.)* I'm not in a position to give you a competent opinion about that.

NORA. Shame on you! *(She lightly brushes his cheek with the stockings in reproof.)* Take that!

> *(She puts them in the box and moves the whole thing up to the table in the corner, right, under the Christmas tree.)*

DOCTOR RANK. And what other wonders am I to see?

NORA. *(Coming down to the right-hand sofa, opposite him.)* You shan't see anything more, because you don't behave nicely...

DOCTOR RANK. *(After a moment, looking at her, savoring the little moment.)* When I sit here this way, talking to you, I can't imagine... I simply can't imagine what would have become of me if I had never entered this house... And now, I have to leave it all.

NORA. Nonsense, you shan't leave us.

DOCTOR RANK. And without leaving behind as much as a little token of gratitude...nothing but some space...the first person that comes along can fill that.

NORA. And just suppose...if I were to ask for you...

DOCTOR RANK. For what?

NORA. For a great proof of your friendship.

DOCTOR RANK. Yes? Yes?

NORA. I mean, for a very, very great service?

DOCTOR RANK. Would you, for once, make me so happy?

NORA. Oh, but you don't know what it is!

DOCTOR RANK. Then tell me!

NORA. No, I really can't, Doctor Rank. It's far too much— not only a service, but help, and advice, besides.

DOCTOR RANK. So much the better. I can't think what it is, but go on. Now, now, don't you trust me?

NORA. I do, indeed, more than I can trust anybody else. I know you're my best and my truest friend. *(She leans in closer to him from the sofa beside his.)* So I will tell you. Doctor Rank, it's something you must help me prevent. You know how deeply, how really deeply Thorwald loves me. He wouldn't hesitate a moment to give his very life for me!

DOCTOR RANK. *(A most simple statement.)* Nora, do you think he's the only one who...?

NORA. What?

DOCTOR RANK. Who would gladly give his life for you?

NORA. Oh!

DOCTOR RANK. I wanted to say it to you once before... I go away. I shall never find a better moment. Yes, Nora, now I've told you. And now you know you can trust me as you can trust no one else.

NORA. *(Utterly upset by this, she rises.)* Doctor Rank!

DOCTOR RANK. Nora...

NORA. *(Crossing up right of the sofas to the vestibule doors, calling into the kitchen.)* Ellen! Ellen, bring in the lamp. *(Returning.)* Oh, dear...Doctor Rank, that was really too bad of you...

DOCTOR RANK. That I have loved someone very deeply? Was that too bad of me?

NORA. No, but that you should have told me so. It wasn't necessary at all.

DOCTOR RANK. *(Rising.)* What do you mean? Did you know?

> *(In the midst of his perplexity,* **ELLEN** *comes in with the lamp for the sofa table. He can't speak before her, and in the little pause that follows,* **NORA** *goes to the table up in the left corner and lights the lamp there.* **ELLEN** *goes back to the kitchen.)*

Nora, I ask you...did you know?

NORA. How can I say what I knew or didn't know? Oh, how could you be so clumsy, Doctor Rank?

(Purely to find something to hide her feelings,
NORA *moves her coat, muff and gloves aimlessly
from the piano bench to the chair left of the piano.)*

NORA. It was all so nice before!

DOCTOR RANK. Well, at any rate, you know now that you
can ask anything of me. And now, go on.

NORA. *(Crosses toward the window, up left, looks unhappily out.)*
Oh, dear…

DOCTOR RANK. I beg you to tell me…what were you going
to ask?

NORA. I can't tell you anything now.

DOCTOR RANK. Yes, yes, you mustn't punish me…not that
way. Let me do for you whatever a man can do.

NORA. No, you can't do anything for me now. *(She moves
from the window.)* Besides, it's not… I really don't want
any help. *(She crosses behind him, in the direction of the
sofas.)* It was just a sort of fancy I had. Yes, that's all it
was. You're a nice one, aren't you? Aren't you ashamed
of yourself…now the lamp's on the table?

DOCTOR RANK. No, not exactly. But perhaps I ought to go
away…for a very long time?

NORA. *(Coming immediately to him.)* No, indeed you mustn't!
Of course, you're to come and go as you've always
done. You know very well Thorwald can't do without
you! *(Barely touching him on the arm as she passes him on
her way to the windows again.)* Oh, you know I always like
to have you here. *(She looks out the lower window.)*

DOCTOR RANK. You are a riddle to me…there have been
times when it seemed that you liked being with me
almost as much as with Helmer.

NORA. *(Walking restlessly past him again, now toward the
vestibule.)* Yes, don't you see? There are people one
loves, and there are others one likes to talk to.

DOCTOR RANK. Yes, there's something in that.

NORA. When I was at home with Papa, of course I loved
Papa best. But I always liked to steal away and go to the
servants' rooms. In the first place, they never lectured

me, and in the second, it was such fun to hear them
talk.

DOCTOR RANK. I see...and it's their place I've taken.

NORA. *(At once she is contrite and approaches him.)* Oh, my
dear Doctor Rank! I didn't mean that at all. But can't
you see? With Thorwald, it's the same as with Papa?

> *(**ELLEN** has come from the kitchen to the living
> room doors.)*

ELLEN. Please, ma'am...

NORA. Yes, Ellen?

> *(**ELLEN** beckons **NORA** to her. She whispers a few
> words to her, then hands her a calling card.)*

Oh...

DOCTOR RANK. *(Sensing something in her tone.)* Anything
wrong?

> *(**ELLEN** turns to go, making her way to the
> kitchen.)*

NORA. Just a moment, Ellen. *(Swiftly coming over to **DOCTOR
RANK**.)* No, of course not. It's just my new costume.

DOCTOR RANK. Your costume? But you said it was in there?
(Indicating her room.)

NORA. Oh, that one, yes! But this is another one...I've
ordered it, and Thorwald mustn't know.

DOCTOR RANK. Ah, so that's the secret?

NORA. Yes, that's the secret. *(Begins moving him toward the
study door.)* Now, Doctor Rank, there is a way that you
can help me; you go in to Thorwald in the study, and
keep him there for a while. You'll think of a way.

> *(**DOCTOR RANK** stops by the study, regarding her
> with a kind of careful tenderness.)*

DOCTOR RANK. Trust me...trust me. *(He knocks, then enters
the study.)*

> *(**NORA** turns back to **ELLEN**, who now waits in
> the vestibule, having just lit the vestibule light.)*

NORA. Is he waiting in the kitchen?

ELLEN. Yes, he came up the back stairs.

NORA. Did you tell him I was busy?

ELLEN. Yes, ma'am.

NORA. Are you sure?

ELLEN. Yes, but it was no use.

NORA. He won't go away?

ELLEN. No, ma'am… I don't think so.

NORA. Then… Ellen, you tell him to come in here. And, Ellen, don't say anything about this.

ELLEN. Yes, ma'am, I understand.

> (**ELLEN** *goes to the kitchen door and beckons to* **KROGSTAD**, *waiting there, out of sight of* **NORA**. **NORA**, *in the living room, stealthily turns the key in the lock to* **HELMER**'s *study door, then moves farther into the living room as* **KROGSTAD** *enters.*)

NORA. *(To* **KROGSTAD**.*)* Speak softly…my husband's at home.

KROGSTAD. All right, that's nothing to me.

NORA. What do you want?

KROGSTAD. I want some information, Mrs. Helmer.

NORA. Be quick, then! What is it?

KROGSTAD. You know I've been dismissed.

NORA. I couldn't prevent it, Mr. Krogstad. I fought and stood up for you, but it wasn't any use.

KROGSTAD. Oh, is that all he cares for you? He knew what I could do, and yet he…

NORA. No, of course he doesn't know about that!

KROGSTAD. I thought not. I wouldn't imagine that my old friend, Thorwald, would have the courage to dismiss me if he'd known everything.

NORA. Mr. Krogstad, you'll kindly speak respectfully of my husband.

KROGSTAD. *(Throws his coat and hat on the big chair left.)* Certainly. You know, Mrs. Helmer, I've been thinking.

I've been thinking about you all day. Even a creature like me has a little bit of what people call feeling, Mrs. Helmer.

NORA. Then show it. Think of my children!

KROGSTAD. Why should I? Did you and your husband think of mine? However!... I've come to tell you that you needn't take this matter too seriously. I'm not going to use this information I've got—not for the present anyway.

NORA. Oh, Mr. Krogstad, I knew you wouldn't!

KROGSTAD. In fact, no one need know. It can remain just between us three.

NORA. Oh, no! My husband must never know.

KROGSTAD. Why, are you ready to pay off the balance?

NORA. Not at the moment, no. But it won't be long before it's all paid, and then...

KROGSTAD. No. Shall I tell you something, Mrs. Helmer? I am going to hold on to that note.

NORA. Why? What would you do with it?

KROGSTAD. Just keep it, Mrs. Helmer.

(**NORA** *crosses to the vestibule doors.*)

Don't worry. No one else will ever know anything about it. So that if you had any desperate scheme in mind, put it right out of your head.

(**NORA** *closes the vestibule doors.*)

If you were thinking, for example, of leaving your husband and the children, or of doing something even more foolish, put such ideas right out of your head. We all think such things at first. I did, too, Mrs. Helmer, but I didn't have the courage.

NORA. (*Returning to the room,* **KROGSTAD** *following her.*) Nor I.

KROGSTAD. No, you wouldn't have the courage, either, would you? It would be very, very foolish, very foolish. Now, I have written a letter to your husband...

NORA. Telling him everything...

KROGSTAD. Sparing you as much as possible.

NORA. He mustn't ever see it. Tear it up! I'll get you the money somehow.

KROGSTAD. I'm sorry, Mrs. Helmer, but I think I've told you…

NORA. Oh, I'm not talking about the money I owe you. How much do you want from my husband? I'll get it!

KROGSTAD. I don't want any money from your husband.

NORA. Then what do you want?

KROGSTAD. I'll tell you what I want. I want to regain my foothold in the world. I want to get back to where I belong. I want to rise!

> (**NORA**, *distracted at his insistence, moves away from him.*)

And your husband shall help me!

NORA. Well, he won't!

KROGSTAD. For the last eighteen months my record has been spotless. At times I've been without money; I've had nothing at all! *(He follows her.)* But I've fought my way back step-by-step. And now I've been pushed down to the bottom again. Well, listen to me! I won't be satisfied to be allowed to sneak back again. I want to rise, I tell you!

NORA. *(Trying to make him keep his voice down.)* Please, Mr. Krogstad!

KROGSTAD. I must get back into the bank again in a higher position than before! Your husband will make a special position for me!

NORA. *(He has her cornered behind the big chair now.)* No, he'll never do that!

KROGSTAD. He will do it! I know him, Mrs. Helmer. He won't dare put up a fight. And when he and I are together there, you'll see!… Yes, within a year, it won't be Thorwald Helmer, it'll be Nils Krogstad who runs the bank.

NORA. *(Facing him squarely.)* No! No!

KROGSTAD. No? Who'll stop me?

NORA. Somebody who has the courage.

KROGSTAD. (*Picking up his hat and coat and turning away from her.*) Ah, you can't frighten me. A petted, pampered creature like you…

NORA. You shall see! You shall see!

KROGSTAD. Under the ice, perhaps? Down in the cold, black water? And next spring to come up again, ugly, unrecognizable? No, no, people don't do that sort of thing, Mrs. Helmer. And, anyway, what would be the use of it? I've got your husband in my pocket, no matter what you do.

(*He struggles into his coat.*)

NORA. Not after I'm gone, after I've…

KROGSTAD. You forget—your reputation remains in my hands. (*He starts for the door, pulling a letter in a blue envelope from his pocket.*) You can think of that while you're planning to do something foolish. As soon as Helmer receives my letter I expect to hear from him. And remember this. It was he who made me go in for this kind of thing, and I shall never forgive him for that. Good evening, Mrs. Helmer.

(*He exits into the vestibule and out the front door of the flat.* **NORA** *rushes toward the vestibule, and we can distinctly hear the lid of the mailbox, on the outside of the door, fall as he drops the letter in.* **NORA** *pauses a moment at the vestibule doors, seizes a hairpin from her head and hurries to the mailbox, futilely trying to pick the lock.*)

(*From* **NORA**'s *room,* **CHRISTINA** *enters with the mended tarantella costume.*)

MRS. LINDEN. There, I think it's all right now. Let's just try it on.

(*She sees nobody in the room.*)

Nora!

(Then she spots **NORA** *in the vestibule.)*

MRS. LINDEN. Why, Nora!

NORA. *(Coming to the vestibule doors.)* Christina! Come here.

MRS. LINDEN. Why, what's the matter, Nora?

NORA. Come here and look! *(She opens the doors wider, and pushes* **CHRISTINA** *past her, for a better view.)* Do you see that letter? There…look through the glass of the mailbox.

MRS. LINDEN. Yes, I see it.

NORA. It's from Krogstad.

MRS. LINDEN. Krogstad?

NORA. *(Coming back into the room, toward the left-hand sofa.)* Yes.

MRS. LINDEN. *(Following her a little.)* So it was Krogstad who lent you the money?

NORA. Yes, and now Thorwald will know everything.

MRS. LINDEN. *(Putting the costume down on the right-hand sofa.)* Believe me, Nora, it will really be best for both of you.

NORA. But you don't know everything yet. I forged a name, I forged Papa's name.

MRS. LINDEN. Good heavens!

NORA. Listen, Christina!—you must witness, you must be my witness…

MRS. LINDEN. "Witness"? What is there to witness?

NORA. If anything should happen, if I should go out of my mind… That could easily happen! Or if…

MRS. LINDEN. Nora!

NORA. If anything should happen so that I wouldn't be here…

MRS. LINDEN. Nora! Nora! You've lost control of yourself!

NORA. If anyone else should try to take the whole blame on himself; you understand what I mean…

MRS. LINDEN. My child, how can you imagine…

NORA. If that should happen, you are my witness that it was all my doing. No one else knew anything about it!

MRS. LINDEN. Nora!

NORA. I'm not out of my mind, Christina; I know what I'm saying. I did the whole thing. You'll remember, won't you?

MRS. LINDEN. Of course I shall remember; but I don't know what you mean!

NORA. No, how could you? Because a very wonderful thing is going to happen. A miracle is going to come.

MRS. LINDEN. A miracle?

NORA. *(Staring straight before her.)* Yes, a wonderful thing. But it's so terrible, too, Christina. It mustn't happen!

> *(She breaks into tears.)*

MRS. LINDEN. *(Going directly into the vestibule for her coat.)* I shall go to Krogstad right now and talk to him.

NORA. No, don't, don't, Christina! He's a terrible man.

MRS. LINDEN. In the old days he would have done anything for me, Nora.

NORA. Krogstad?

MRS. LINDEN. *(Pinning on her hat, she hurries back into the room.)* Where does he live?

NORA. How should I know? *(Remembering.)* Oh, yes, yes, here's his card! *(She digs it out of her belt where she had stuffed it.)* But there's that letter!

HELMER. *(Inside his study, rattling the locked door.)* Nora!

> *(**CHRISTINA** hurries to the coat tree for her coat.)*

NORA. *(Answering **HELMER**.)* What? What is it? What do you want?

HELMER. *(Still locked out.)* Well, well, don't be frightened. We're not coming in, you've locked the door. Are you trying on your costume?

NORA. Yes, Thorwald, we're trying it on. It's just right. It fits me perfectly, Thorwald!

MRS. LINDEN. *(Coming back into the room with her coat on.)* Why, he lives just a few steps away.

NORA. Yes, but that won't help. There's that letter!

MRS. LINDEN. *(Starting out.)* Well, get it out!

NORA. But Thorwald has the only key!

MRS. LINDEN. Then, listen, Nora! Krogstad must come here and ask for his letter back, unread! He must think of some reason!

NORA. But the letter box! This is the time that Thorwald usually goes to open it!

MRS. LINDEN. Don't let him! Keep him occupied! I'll be back as quickly as I can!

> (**CHRISTINA** *rushes out the front door.* **NORA,** *making an effort to pull herself together, unlocks the study door and moves away from it, with a sudden assumption of bright gaiety.)*

NORA. Thorwald!

HELMER. *(Opening the study doors and entering,* **DOCTOR RANK** *behind him.)* Well, can I come back into my own home again, at last? Come in, Rank, we'll have a look at... Why, what's happened? Rank told me I was to see a dazzling transformation!

DOCTOR RANK. *(In the doorway, sensing, much better than* **HELMER,** *that something is wrong.)* Yes, so I was told.

NORA. No. No one shall see me in my costume until tomorrow night!

HELMER. Why, Nora, what's the matter? Have you been practicing too hard?

NORA. No, I haven't practiced at all yet!

HELMER. But you'll have to.

NORA. I certainly will. I must practice a great deal. But, Thorwald, I can't without you! I know I've forgotten everything.

HELMER. Oh, well, we'll work on it and it'll come back to you.

NORA. Yes, Thorwald, you'll have to help me. You must promise...

> (*She clings to him, in an anxiety out of all*

proportion to her concern for her dance.)

I'm really terrified when I think of all those people watching! Now, tonight, you must give up everything you're doing—for me! You mustn't do a stroke of work. You mustn't even touch a pen! Promise me that, Thorwald!

HELMER. All right, I promise. I'll be your slave the whole evening...my poor, helpless child.

(He turns away, heading for the vestibule doors.)

NORA. *(After him.)* Where are you going?

HELMER. *(Held by her.)* Only to have a look at the mailbox.

NORA. No, no, don't do that!

HELMER. Why not?

NORA. Thorwald, I'm sure there are no letters there.

HELMER. Let me just look...

*(Taking a bunch of keys from his pocket, he strolls into the vestibule. **NORA** rushes to the table up right, seizes her tambourine and shakes it.)*

NORA. If you don't rehearse with me, I won't be able to dance tomorrow!

HELMER. *(At the mailbox now, fumbling with the lock.)* What? You're really as nervous about it as all that?

NORA. *(Putting down the tambourine and running into the vestibule to drag him away from the mailbox.)* Terribly! Thorwald! Let's rehearse now! There's time before dinner!

(She has him by the arm and pulls him back into the room, toward the piano.)

Sit down and play for me, Thorwald! And you know what you can do? You can direct me, you know, the way you used to do!

HELMER. *(At once flattered and indulgent.)* All right, all right... Oh, what a creature it is!

(He plays the opening bar of the dance, and pauses,

laughing, to pat **NORA** *on the cheek.* **NORA** *runs for her tambourine.)*

HELMER. What a creature!

NORA. Play, Thorwald, play!

> *(She takes the opening position of her dance, to the right of the piano, seeking, with the utmost concentration, to keep* **HELMER** *involved in this charade as long as possible. He plays vigorously, as* **NORA** *whirls in the first movements she learned so long ago, dancing, in her nervousness, out of time with the music.)*

HELMER. Slower! Slower!

NORA. Can't do it any slower!

HELMER. Not so violently, Nora!

NORA. I must!

> *(His artistic soul outrages,* **HELMER** *leaves the piano.)*

HELMER. That will never do.

NORA. *(Seeing him move vaguely toward the mailbox, she is right after him.)* Thorwald, please! I told you I needed to practice!

DOCTOR RANK. *(Missing nothing of any of this, he goes to the piano himself.)* Let me play for her. Perhaps we can do it slower.

NORA. Oh, please! *(She shepherds* **HELMER** *down to the left-hand sofa, seats him.)* Now look, Thorwald, sit here and then you watch me!

HELMER. All right, all right. Try to calm yourself!

NORA. *(Running breathlessly up left of the piano, and once again striking her opening pose for the dance.)* I will, darling!

> *(***DOCTOR RANK** *plays. He is in the introduction music when* **CHRISTINA**, *returning from* **KROGSTAD**'s *house, hurries into the room from the outer door and vestibule.)*

Christina! We're having such fun here!

(Her cue in the music is reached, she dances.
HELMER, *in the splendid conceit of an amateur of*
the dance, beats time with his hands and hums the
tune. **NORA** *dances three figures of the dance at an*
intensity far beyond her strength. She is entering
the fourth, and **DOCTOR RANK**, *strangely infected*
by her, is increasing the tempo until **HELMER** *finds*
the whole thing wrong again, and rises to stop it.)

HELMER. Nora, there's no need to dance as though it were a matter of life and death! Rank, stop! This is all out of control! Stop, I say!

*(**DOCTOR RANK** stops.)*

I don't see how you could have forgotten everything that way!

NORA. *(Breathless from her exertions.)* I told you I had. Oh, Thorwald, you must practice with me right up to the last minute. Promise, Thorwald!

HELMER. Certainly, if you wish.

NORA. Neither today nor tomorrow are you to think of anything but me! Not a letter, not a paper...you mustn't even look at the mailbox!

HELMER. Oh, you're still afraid of that man...

NORA. Yes, I am.

HELMER. *(Playfully teasing her.)* I can see it in your face; there's a letter in the mailbox now.

NORA. Perhaps there is, I don't know. But you're not to read it now. Nothing...nothing! Must come into this house until my dance is over tomorrow night!

DOCTOR RANK. *(Who has risen from the piano, closely attending every desperate shift in* **NORA**'*s hysteria.)* You mustn't contradict her.

(He walks away from them, right.)

HELMER. Very well. My child shall have her own way until tomorrow night.

*(**ELLEN** enters the vestibule from the dining room*

door and comes to the living room doors.)

ELLEN. The dinner is on the table, ma'am.

NORA. *(Breaking away from* **HELMER**, *saved for the time by this announcement.)* Then you'll be free to do as you like. We'll have champagne, too, Ellen!

ELLEN. Yes, ma'am.

HELMER. Well, it's quite a banquet!

NORA. And we'll keep it up until morning. And macaroons, Ellen!

> *(***ELLEN*** bows and returns to the dining room.*
> **NORA** *turns to* **HELMER**, *placating him for her dissipation.)*

Lots of them…just this once!

HELMER. Now, now, don't let's get excited. Be a nice little girl.

NORA. Oh, I will, I will. Go on into the dining room. You go, too, Doctor Rank…*(The men start off; she moves left, toward her friend.)* Christina, help me with my hair…

DOCTOR RANK. *(On the way out; quietly to* **HELMER**.*)* There's nothing wrong, is there? Nothing, I mean…

HELMER. Oh, nothing of the sort. It's just this childish anxiety I was telling you about.

> *(They cross into the vestibule and out to the dining room.)*

> *(***NORA*** is at last free to ask* **CHRISTINA** *her question.)*

NORA. Well?

MRS. LINDEN. He wasn't there.

NORA. I could see it in your face.

MRS. LINDEN. I left him a note.

NORA. You shouldn't have done that, Christina. *(With the deepest conviction.)* What must be, must be. And after all, Christina, there's something almost glorious about waiting for the miracle to come.

MRS. LINDEN. What is it you're waiting for?

NORA. You wouldn't understand, Christina. You go in to the others. Go on, darling, I'll come in a minute!

(*She almost pushes* **CHRISTINA** *away from her, out the door, then returns, alone, to the place behind her husband's chair, seeing everything now most clearly.*)

Seven o'clock...five hours to midnight, twenty-four hours till the next midnight, then the tarantella will be over. Twenty-four and five...twenty-nine hours to live.

HELMER. (*Emerging from the Christmas feast in the dining room to bring her in.*) What's become of my little girl?

NORA. (*Turning away for an instant to summon all the spiritual energy she has, before she races, in her old, lighthearted manner, into his arms.*) Here she is, Thorwald!

(*The curtain slowly falls.*)

ACT THREE

(The same room, the evening of the day after Christmas. The lamps are lighted, the doors to the nursery and Helmer's study are closed. The doors to the vestibule are open.)

(From upstairs, where the party is going on at Consul Stenborg's, drifts the sound of a waltz.)

*(**CHRISTINA** is sitting on the right-hand sofa. She is knitting. She has perhaps been there alone for some time, for now she drops her hands, looks once toward the door, presses her eyes, gets up, and walks aimlessly, restlessly, up to the piano. She puts down her knitting, picks up a book lying there, looks again toward the door, then at the watch pinned on her bosom.)*

(She moves toward the window. Looking out into the night, she sees a man coming up the street, below. She follows him with her eyes, sees him with her mind's eye pass the front of the house, and is at once galvanized into action when she hears the street door slam. She hurries across the room, then into the vestibule to leave the outer door of the flat off the latch. Returning to the living room, she picks up the book, sits on the left-hand sofa, and tries to compose herself into an image of a person who has not been waiting for somebody.)

*(**KROGSTAD** comes into the vestibule, staring at her through the glass, in an agony of distress, reluctance, uncertainty.)*

MRS. LINDEN. Come in! There's nobody here but me.

(KROGSTAD stands at the vestibule doors now, steadily, miserably, regarding her.)

KROGSTAD. You left a note at my house.

MRS. LINDEN. Yes, I wanted to see you. Come in.

(He is just inside the doors, but not moving.)

I couldn't ask you to come to my lodgings at this hour, otherwise...

KROGSTAD. What do you want?

MRS. LINDEN. *(As smiling and charming as possible.)* Do sit down, Krogstad. Please! We're quite alone. The servants are asleep, and Nora and Thorwald are upstairs at the ball.

KROGSTAD. *(Hearing the music upstairs; totally without expression.)* Ah, they're dancing. How nice.

MRS. LINDEN. Yes, isn't it? And now let's have a little talk.

KROGSTAD. Why did you ask me to come here?

MRS. LINDEN. I just told you...my lodgings are...

KROGSTAD. Yes, but why here?

MRS. LINDEN. Why not? No one will disturb us, there's nothing to be afraid of. Sit down, Krogstad, please!

(Slowly, still hesitant, he comes down and sits in the sofa at her right, hat in hand, looking at her.)

Well, Krogstad, have you nothing to say to me?

KROGSTAD. I don't think so.

MRS. LINDEN. You're very cruel. It's a pity you never understood me, Krogstad.

KROGSTAD. What was there to understand? It wasn't the first time a woman threw a man over for a better match.

MRS. LINDEN. Did you think it was easy for me to give you up?

KROGSTAD. It couldn't have been very hard.

MRS. LINDEN. Krogstad!

KROGSTAD. *(His voice beginning to get out of control.)* How could you have written me that letter?

MRS. LINDEN. *(Moving nearer to him, on her sofa.)* Shhh!

KROGSTAD. That cold, curt letter, breaking everything off, refusing to see me!

MRS. LINDEN. Krogstad, you must not shout! The children are sleeping! Listen, wasn't that the best way after all, since I had to do it? Shouldn't I have tried to put an end to your feeling for me?

KROGSTAD. All for the sake of money.

MRS. LINDEN. Yes, I had a family to think of.

KROGSTAD. So you think it was right to cast me off as you did.

MRS. LINDEN. I don't know, Krogstad, I don't know. I've often asked myself the same question.

KROGSTAD. *(Leaning back, smiling, almost masochistic as he regards the wreckage of himself.)* Well, you see what it did to me. Look at me, I am a completely shipwrecked man.

MRS. LINDEN. Perhaps there is something at hand for you to cling to.

KROGSTAD. There was something, but you came and took it away.

MRS. LINDEN. Nils, I never dreamed! It was only today that I found out it was your place I was taking in the bank!

KROGSTAD. I don't doubt it. And now that you have found out, are you stepping aside for me?

MRS. LINDEN. No, because that wouldn't help you. Nils... there's something I've learned from life. That is, not to be stupid.

KROGSTAD. Well, I've learned something, too...not to trust fine speeches!

MRS. LINDEN. Then you have learned a very sensible thing. But actions you will trust?

KROGSTAD. What do you mean?

MRS. LINDEN. You say you're shipwrecked. I am shipwrecked, too. I have no one in the world to care for!

KROGSTAD. You made your choice.

MRS. LINDEN. I had no choice. Nils, what if we two shipwrecked people were to join hands?

> (**KROGSTAD** *simply looks at her.*)

Nils, suppose we could help save each other?

> (*With great urgency, she extends her hands toward him*)

What do you think brought me here?

> (*Overwhelmed by his mingled feelings of hatred, of despair, of unbelief,* **KROGSTAD** *breaks into tears, even now trying to hide his face from her, behind his hands.*)

Nils, listen to me, please! Living doesn't mean anything to me unless I can be working, and working for some person. My whole life, as far back as I can remember, I've been working in that way. It's been my only happiness. Now, I'm alone in the world. I have no one to care for, and no one to care what I'm doing. Nils! Give me something to work for!

KROGSTAD. (*Quite broken by this.*) No, no, that's impossible.

MRS. LINDEN. Why, Nils?

KROGSTAD. It's just some notion of yours—a romantic craving for self-sacrifice.

MRS. LINDEN. Have you ever found me romantic?

KROGSTAD. Christina! You don't know the things I've done!

MRS. LINDEN. Perhaps I do.

KROGSTAD. And what people say about me…

MRS. LINDEN. You would have been a different man with me.

KROGSTAD. Yes…I know.

MRS. LINDEN. (*Coming to him, literally on her knees.*) Is it too late, then? Nils, you're still young. We can both…

KROGSTAD. Christina! Do you know what you're doing?

> (*She smiles at him with great and grave confidence.*)

Yes, you do! I can almost believe it. But have you the courage?

MRS. LINDEN. I have the need...a great need, for someone to care for! And that gives me courage. I'm not afraid with you.

KROGSTAD. Oh, Christina, I'm so grateful, so grateful!

(He presses her hands to his face. Upstairs, at the party, the waltz has stopped. The piano begins the introductory music to NORA's tarantella.)

There's still time for us to make up for what's lost. Our whole lives...

(CHRISTINA realizes that NORA's part of the evening's entertainment will soon be coming to an end. She rises.)

MRS. LINDEN. Shhh! The tarantella! You'll have to go!

(She hurries toward the vestibule. KROGSTAD, startled, gets up, sidles upstage between the sofas and the vestibule, like a thief caught where he has no right to be.)

KROGSTAD. Why? What is it?

MRS. LINDEN. Listen! As soon as that's over, they'll be here!

KROGSTAD. Who?

MRS. LINDEN. Nora and Thorwald. They'll come right down!

KROGSTAD. All right, I'll go. *(He moves to the vestibule, and is stopped dead by his thought.)* Oh, God, I forgot! You don't know what I've done to them.

MRS. LINDEN. Yes, Nils, I do know.

KROGSTAD. Oh, if there was only something I could do!

MRS. LINDEN. Your letter is still in the box.

KROGSTAD. Are you sure?

MRS. LINDEN. *(Drawing him through the vestibule doors, she shows him the mailbox.)* There it is.

KROGSTAD. *(The whole bright texture of his new joy is broken.)* Ah, now I understand! You wanted to save your friend!

MRS. LINDEN. Nils!

KROGSTAD. That's what was behind everything you said tonight!

MRS. LINDEN. No, no!

KROGSTAD. You wanted to bring me around!

MRS. LINDEN. *(Who needs belief, as much as he needs to believe.)* Nils, a woman doesn't sell herself twice. Trust me, Nils!

KROGSTAD. *(Who must accept what she is offering.)* All right, I'll demand my letter back again. Yes, of course! I'll wait till Helmer comes. I'll tell him to give it back to me, that it's only about my dismissal, that I don't want it read!

MRS. LINDEN. *(Who sees more clearly than anybody at this point what must be done.)* No, Nils, no.

KROGSTAD. Or better still, I can force it out with my pocket knife. That would be so much better.

> *(He is practically reaching into his pocket for the knife when she seizes his arm.)*

MRS. LINDEN. No, Nils, wait! You mustn't.

KROGSTAD. But wasn't that just why you got me to come here?

MRS. LINDEN. Yes, at first. But a day has passed since then, and in that day I've seen incredible things in this house. Sooner or later Thorwald will have to know everything.

KROGSTAD. But why, if I take back my letter?

MRS. LINDEN. There must be an end to that wretched secret. Those two must come to an understanding. They can't possibly go on with all these lies and evasions!

KROGSTAD. *(Who knows **HELMER** better than she does.)* Very well, if you want to risk it!

MRS. LINDEN. *(Hearing the applause for **NORA** upstairs.)* Hurry! Quick! The dance is over… We're not safe another moment!

KROGSTAD. I'll wait for you in the street.

MRS. LINDEN. Yes, yes, you must take me home.

KROGSTAD. *(As transfigured as he ever will be.)* Christina, listen! I've never been so happy in my life!

> *(Upstairs, the door to the Stenborg flat is opened, and the party voices are heard for a moment. The door closes. The sound of **NORA** and **HELMER** coming downstairs.)*

MRS. LINDEN. *(Pushing him out the front door.)* They're coming!

> *(Confused, she hurries back into the living room for an instant, hears **NORA** and **HELMER** in the hall, comes out to the coat tree for her hat, and returns to the living room, to the mirror on the piano, to put it on.*
>
> *Protesting, **NORA** still in her character of the willful "creature," but with the undertones of a really final urgency. The two of them, man and wife, are outside their own door.)*

NORA. No, no, I won't go in! I want to go upstairs again! I don't want to leave so early!

HELMER. *(Talking through and over her pleas, jovial and authoritative.)* But, my dearest girl!

NORA. Oh, please, please, Thorwald!

HELMER. Come now, it's cold out here...there's a draft in this corridor. You promised...

NORA. Please, Thorwald, only one hour more!

> *(Upstairs, the party resumes, with another waltz, drifting into and through the scene.)*

HELMER. Not one more minute. Come...come in!

> *(He pulls her through the vestibule, then into the living room. He wears a black satin cape, the lapels faced with black and white, and a fantastically inappropriate red satin cap with pointed horns. He is all laughter and good spirits.)*

Look what we have here! Rebellion!

(He has had just enough champagne to know there is someone in the room, but to know or care not quite who it can be.)

MRS. LINDEN. Good evening…

NORA. Christina!

HELMER. Oh, it's you. Good evening, Mrs. Linden. You here so late?

MRS. LINDEN. I just missed you when I came. I couldn't go away without seeing Nora.

HELMER. *(Proudly moving* **NORA** *into the center of the room.)* Behold! There's something to look at. Isn't she marvelous?

MRS. LINDEN. Yes, I must say…

HELMER. Isn't she a beauty? Everybody said so tonight. But she's terribly obstinate; obstinate, adorable, childish, dear little creature! What's to be done with her? I had to carry her off by force, Mrs. Linden!

(He pats **NORA**'s *shoulder affectionately, and now she moves away from him, to the piano bench.)*

There she danced the tarantella. Great success! Deserved, too, though she did put a little too much, you know, realism into it. But never mind! It was a great success, Mrs. Linden, a tremendous success. What was I to let her do after that? Let her stay there and talk to this person and that and weaken the impression? No, not if I know what's right!

(In his exuberance, he pantomimes the gracefulness of his farewells upstairs.) So I took my adorable little Nora under my arm, a quick turn around the room: "Good night, Good night, Good night!" *(He has* **NORA**'s *tambourine in his hand and now pivots quite completely around, bowing himself out of the imaginary room.)* And as they say in novels, the lovely apparition vanished. *(He lays down the tambourine on the table.)* An exit should always be effective, Mrs. Linden, but I can't get Nora to see it.

(Tired by his own histrionic skill.) My, it's warm in here. *(He goes up and opens his study doors.)* What, no lights in here? Excuse me, Mrs. Linden.

> *(He exits, closing his study door after him.* **MRS. LINDEN***, who has listened politely to* **HELMER** *while attending mostly to* **NORA***'s quiet, sinister absorption, comes and sits beside her on the piano bench.)*

MRS. LINDEN. I've spoken to him... Nora, you must tell your husband everything! You have nothing to fear from Krogstad, but you must speak out!

NORA. *(Simply shaking her head.)* No, I shan't speak.

MRS. LINDEN. Then the letter will.

> **(HELMER** *reenters from his study. He has removed his fancy dress and wears his smoking jacket over his dress shirt.)*

HELMER. Well, Mrs. Linden, have you admired her?

MRS. LINDEN. Yes, very much. And now I'll say good night.

> *(She heads into the vestibule for her coat.* **HELMER***, still pleasantly aglow with wine, picks up the knitting from off the piano.)*

HELMER. What, so soon? Oh, does this knitting belong to you?

MRS. LINDEN. Yes, thanks. I was nearly forgetting it.

HELMER. Then you do knit?

MRS. LINDEN. Yes.

HELMER. Do you know what you should do? You should embroider!

MRS. LINDEN. *(Returning to the room, coat on, gloves and bag in her hand.)* Indeed? Why?

HELMER. *(Giving her the knitting.)* Because it's so much prettier. Look now! You hold the embroidery in the left hand, so! Then you work the needle with the right hand, in long, graceful curves. Isn't that right?

> *(In his enthusiasm, he gives a good imitation of a woman embroidering.)*

MRS. LINDEN. Yes, I suppose so.

HELMER. But knitting is always ugly. Look now, your arms close to your sides, and the needles going up and down, up and down…*(He observes his own motions and makes a discovery.)* Why, there's something Chinese about it! *(He strolls lazily to his chair.)* They really gave us marvelous champagne tonight.

> *(He sits.)*

MRS. LINDEN. *(Coming to the piano bench, to **NORA**, who all this time has not moved, has not even listened.)* Well, good night, Nora, and don't be obstinate anymore.

HELMER. *(Absentmindedly approving this splendid advice.)* Well said, Mrs. Linden.

MRS. LINDEN. Good night, Mr. Helmer. *(She goes into the vestibule, opens the outer door for herself.)*

HELMER. Good night. I hope you'll get safely home. *(Suddenly realizing his duties as a host.)* I should be glad to…but really…*(He rises and crosses after her into the vestibule.)* You haven't far to go, Mrs. Linden. Good night, good night, good night.

> *(In the living room, **NORA** slowly rises and comes and seats herself in the right-hand sofa. **HELMER**, in the vestibule, bolts the outer door, sighs with self-satisfaction and champagne, and turns out the vestibule light.)*

Well, she's gone at last. She's an awful bore.

> *(He returns to the living room, closing the doors after him.)*

NORA. Aren't you tired, Thorwald?

HELMER. Not in the least!

NORA. Nor sleepy?

HELMER. Never felt livelier in my life. What's the matter with you? You do look tired and sleepy.

NORA. Yes, I am. I shall sleep soon.

HELMER. *(Absently, satisfying the orderliness of his nature, he picks up her tambourine from the table where he left it, and*

puts it on the table, under the Christmas tree.) There, you
see? I was perfectly right not to let you stay any longer.

NORA. *(It is impossible to understand just how she means this.)*
Yes, everything you do is right. *(After she has said it, it
could be that she means it absolutely)*

HELMER. *(Coming to sit beside her.)* Ah, that sounds better,
much better. Did you notice how gay Rank was tonight?

NORA. Was he?

HELMER. *(Sitting down and putting an easy arm around her.)* I
haven't seen him in such high spirits for a long time.
Oh, it's such a relief to be home again. *(In a warm,
sensual enjoyment of the moment, he pulls her even nearer to
him.)* Oh, you enchanting thing, you...

NORA. Don't...

HELMER. But why not? Aren't you mine, all mine, every bit
of you?

> *(He slips her shawl off her shoulders, almost
> voluptuously. She is in her tarantella dress, all
> white, and old rose—childishly, dearly attractive
> to him. He feels a sly secretiveness about their
> isolation, in their warm home, in this holiday
> pause in the serious affairs of his life. He is
> contented and sure, and he wants her.)*

NORA. Not tonight, please.

HELMER. Ah, I know what it is. You have the tarantella still
in your blood...makes you all the more tempting. *(He
holds her closer, and listens, for an instant, to the waltzing as
it comes faintly into his consciousness from upstairs.)* Shhh!
Hear them upstairs? They'll be breaking up soon, and
the whole house will be still again. Listen, Nora, I have
a secret to tell you. Do you know why I'm so distant to
you when there are people around? Do you notice how
I keep away off, and only now and then steal a glance
at you? Do you know why I do that? Shhh! It's because
I'm pretending to myself that we love each other in
secret, no one knows that there's anything between us,
it's a secret.

NORA. Yes, I know that you're thinking about me.

HELMER. And then when the party's over, and I put the shawl about your shoulders and your adorable neck, then I think to myself that it's like…it's as though we had just been married and I was taking you back to your home for the first time. All evening tonight I watched you, while you whirled and swayed in the tarantella, and I was longing for you, until I could scarcely bear it any longer. And that's why I made you come home with me so early.

> *(Inflamed, and in his own way deeply moved by his imaginings, he tries to draw her even closer.)*

NORA. No, Thorwald, do go away a little. I won't have all this nonsense.

HELMER. Nonsense? What do you mean? Oh, I see, you're joking. So you won't have any nonsense? Well, after all, I'm your husband, aren't I?

> *(Persuading himself easily this is only another of her moods, he tries to kiss her. She pushes against him, and there is heard, suddenly, the sharp tapping of* **DOCTOR RANK**'s *cane on the door of their flat.)*

NORA. What's that?

HELMER. Who's there?

DOCTOR RANK. *(Just outside the outer door, his voice only slightly heard.)* It's I…

HELMER. *(Unwillingly rising.)* What the devil does he want to call now for?

DOCTOR RANK. May I come in for a minute?

HELMER. Wait a minute.

> *(Forced to be the social being for the time, he goes out into the vestibule and unlocks the outer door.)*

(All hearty welcome now.) Come in, come in! Very nice of you to drop in on us!

(He closes the door after **DOCTOR RANK,** *who comes carefully, neatly, like a man knowing his every footstep, into the living room. He passes behind* **NORA** *and walks left, almost to the big chair.* **HELMER** *follows him into the room, and comes to stand behind his seated wife.* **DOCTOR RANK** *has condescended to the party upstairs to the extent of getting into full dress. To this he has added an opera cape, lined with white satin. Over his eyes he wears a thin slit of a gold domino. He carries his cane, and depends on it a little, because he, too, has had champagne, and he, alone, is aware of what is closing in on him.)*

DOCTOR RANK. I thought I heard your voices, so it occurred to me to look in on you...*(He half turns his head toward them, taking in the domestic scene.)* How cozy you two are in here...

HELMER. You seemed to like it upstairs, too.

DOCTOR RANK. Yes, I enjoyed myself. And why not? Why not take one's share of whatever's going on in this world? All one can...and as long as one can. *(He lifts his mask off his eyes, up onto his forehead.)* The wine was splendid.

HELMER. Especially the champagne.

(Upstairs, the party has reached its closing phase, and someone begins singing, blurred by the separating walls and masonry, a simple country song.)

DOCTOR RANK. You noticed it, too? I can scarcely believe myself how much of it I managed to get down.

NORA. Thorwald had a good deal, too.

(Disembodied from the scene, she rises, drifting, like someone not there, over to the left, into the shadows beyond **HELMER**'s *chair.)*

DOCTOR RANK. Did he?

NORA. Yes, and as usual it put him into very good spirits.

DOCTOR RANK. Well, why not? Why shouldn't one have a lively evening after a well-spent day?

HELMER *(Who has comfortably sat himself down in the place left vacant by* **NORA**.*)* Well-spent? Well, I can't boast about that exactly.

DOCTOR RANK. *(With the utmost simple seriousness.)* But, you see, I can.

NORA. I suppose you did some important scientific investigation?

DOCTOR RANK. I did.

HELMER. Listen to the creature! Talking about scientific investigations!

NORA. Am I to congratulate you on the result?

DOCTOR RANK. You may, indeed.

NORA. *(Still standing alone, shadowed, not looking at him.)* It was good, then?

DOCTOR RANK. Perfect. Absolutely perfect. Both for doctor and patient. I arrived at a certainty. *(He has all the calm of a man already dead.)* Absolute certainty. So wasn't I right to enjoy myself tonight?

NORA. Yes, quite right, Doctor Rank.

HELMER. *(Very merry, still on the right-hand sofa.)* That's what I say! Always, of course, on condition that you don't have to pay for it tomorrow.

DOCTOR RANK. *(Quite peacefully and exactly.)* In this life, nothing can be had for nothing, exactly.

NORA. You like masquerade parties, don't you, Doctor Rank?

DOCTOR RANK. Yes; oh, yes, especially when there are plenty of comical disguises.

NORA. What shall you and I be at our next masquerade?

HELMER. *(Heartily laughing.)* Ho! She's thinking of the next party already!

DOCTOR RANK. We two? Let me see... You are to go as a good fairy.

HELMER. *(To whom this seems a capital idea.)* Good! And what shall she wear to show that?

DOCTOR RANK. Why, simply her everyday dress.

HELMER. Her everyday dress. Splendid! And you?

DOCTOR RANK. Oh, I know very well what I shall be.

HELMER. What?

DOCTOR RANK. At the next masquerade, I shall be invisible.

HELMER. *(Overcome, the fellow is really too resourceful.)* Glorious!!

DOCTOR RANK. *(In deadly earnest.)* There's a big black hat... Have you heard about the invisible hat? It comes down all over you...

> *(He raises both his arms, pantomiming this hat, drawing his arms down across his face, his eyes closing, his arms crossing over his breast, relaxing, dropping to his sides.)*

...like this! And no one can see you.

HELMER. *(His pleasure in the inventiveness of his friend now out of all bounds.)* Perfect, absolutely perfect! You're in magnificent form tonight, old fellow!

DOCTOR RANK. *(Opening his eyes.)* But I'm forgetting what I came for. Helmer, give me a cigar.

HELMER. It's a pleasure, my dear fellow.

> *(He goes up into his study, for a moment going out of sight.)*

DOCTOR RANK. One of those long, dark, fragrant Havanas.

> *(Slowly, he turns and looks at **NORA**. **NORA** smiles at him, a strange smile, compounded of the close understanding of death she now shares with him. **HELMER** comes out of the study with a long Havana cigar.)*

HELMER. Here you are, my dear fellow.

DOCTOR RANK. Thank you. Thank you very much.

> *(**DOCTOR RANK** takes the cigar. He removes a gold*

cigar cutter from his pocket and, precisely, like a
man savoring an experience for the last time, snips
off the end.)

HELMER. Let me give you a light.

(**HELMER** *takes out his matches and strikes one.*
He holds the light to **DOCTOR RANK**'s *cigar.*
DOCTOR RANK, *to steady himself, holds onto*
HELMER's *hands, lifting himself to his full height,*
all the while drawing in the cigar, tasting the
tobacco, all of this a farewell to the house. He expels
the fragrant smoke in a great breath.)

DOCTOR RANK. Many thanks. And now…good-bye.

(*He turns toward the vestibule.*)

HELMER. (*Standing aside, watching with manly amusement*
his friend's drunkenness.) Good-bye, good-bye, my dear
fellow.

NORA. (*Who, at last, when* **HELMER** *left for his study, had to*
sit, on the little chair, down left, as she understood completely
the purport of **DOCTOR RANK**'s *visit.*) Sleep well, Doctor
Rank.

DOCTOR RANK. (*On his way out.*) Thank you for the wish.

NORA. Wish me the same.

DOCTOR RANK. (*Almost at the vestibule now, he turns.*) You?
Very well. Sleep well. (*He enters the vestibule.*) And thanks
for the light!

(*He is gone.*)

HELMER. (*Having no other explanation for this mysterious,*
foreboding exit.) He's been drinking a good deal tonight.

(*He goes off into the vestibule, to close the outer*
door, to pick up the threads of his daily routine, to
find in it some escape from the strange reality that
has come close to him.)

NORA. Thorwald, what are you doing?

HELMER. I want to clear out the mailbox. It's full. There
won't be any room for the morning papers.

(We can hear him, with his keys, at the lock.)

NORA. Are you going to work tonight?

HELMER. Not very likely. *(He discovers something wrong with the lock.)* Hm? Somebody's been at this lock.

NORA. At the lock?

HELMER. I'm sure of it. Well, this is mysterious! I can't believe the servants would…

NORA. What is it?

HELMER. *(He has found an odd thing.)* A broken hairpin. Nora, it's one of yours.

> **(HELMER** *opens the box at last. He picks up a pile of letters and comes back into the room.)*

Well, you must certainly see that the children get over tricks like that. *(He sets down the letters on the sofa table, picks a calling card off the top.)* Look at all the letters that have collected. Why, what's this?

NORA. What?

HELMER. This black cross over his name. Look! What a ghastly idea! You'd think he was announcing his own death.

NORA. He is.

HELMER. What? Do you know anything? Has he told you something?

NORA. That card is his farewell. He's going to shut himself up alone and die.

HELMER. Poor old boy! Of course, I knew we couldn't hope to keep him long. *(Now quite at a loss, he drops into his chair.)* But so soon! And to go and creep off alone, like a wounded animal…

NORA. When one goes, it's best to go silently. Don't you think so, Thorwald?

HELMER. I just can't realize he's gone. He'd grown into our lives so. He was like a cloud that was always there. Somehow, with his illness, and his loneliness… And our happiness was the silver lining.

*(**NORA** gets up from her chair, moves to the left of him, more in the shadow than ever, and stands staring out the window into the cold night. **HELMER** uneasily, not wanting this intrusion of a sad fact, snaps the card with his finger.)*

HELMER. Well, perhaps it's for the best...at least for him. *(He rises, comes behind **NORA**.)* And for us, too, because now we'll have to depend entirely on each other. *(He puts his arms around her.)* Oh, my darling, I just can't hold you close enough. You know, I wish sometimes you were in some great trouble, so that I could do something really marvelous for you—risk my body and soul—everything! Everything!

NORA. *(She disengages herself gently.)* Now you must read your letters, Thorwald.

HELMER. *(He clings to her again.)* No, no, not tonight. I want to be with my little wife...

NORA. No...

HELMER. *(Turning, puzzled, as she moves away from him.)* But, why not, my darling?

NORA. *(Walking farther away from him.)* Because of poor Rank...the thought of that...

(This is, now, the best excuse she can think of.)

HELMER. Yes, you're right. It's a queer thing...the way that news has come between us. But later on we must keep such thoughts out of our heads.

(He moves toward her.)

NORA. *(Putting her arms around him.)* Thorwald! Good night, good night!

HELMER. *(Kissing her.)* Good night, my little songbird. Sleep well.

(He starts away from her; she abruptly embraces him again. He kisses her a second time, faintly surprised at so much warmth. He pats her gently and goes over to the sofa table, picking up his pile of mail.)

HELMER. Now I'll go and look into my letters.

> *(With the mail in his hand,* **KROGSTAD** *'s blue envelope plainly visible, he goes over to the vestibule doors and closes them, shooting the bolt. He stops by the sofa table and blows out the lamp. He goes into his study, closing the door after him.* **NORA,** *alone in her house, takes her inevitable final look about her. Knowing what she must do, she dismisses it all with a look, starts right, takes her shawl from the sofa, and goes to the vestibule doors. She is pulling back the bold when* **HELMER** *speaks.)*

HELMER. *(From inside the study)* Nora!

> *(Businesslike, he has started through his mail from top to bottom and has opened, and glanced at,* **KROGSTAD** *'s letter first.* **NORA** *is opening the door and starting into the vestibule, when he bursts out of the study.)*

HELMER. What is this? Do you know what's in this letter?

NORA. *(It is all she can say or think.)* Let me go! Let me out!

HELMER. *(Coming into the vestibule after her, seizing her by the arm.)* Wait! Where are you going? Answer me!

NORA. I've loved you more than anything else in the world!

HELMER. Nora, answer me! Is this true?

NORA. It was all because I loved you!

HELMER. Stop saying that! Stop these evasions and answer me!

NORA. *(He has dragged her back almost to the living room doors now.)* Yes, it's true, Thorwald.

HELMER. You fool! What have you done?

NORA. Thorwald, you're not going to take this on yourself! You're not to try to save me!

HELMER. *(Pulling her farther into the room.)* Don't be melodramatic! Where is it you're trying to go?

> *(He flings her past him, the impetus carries her to the center of the room, and she falls on the piano bench.)*

HELMER. You stay right here and give an account of yourself! Do you understand what you've done? Answer me! Do you understand it?

NORA. *(Her face quite muffled in her arms.)* Yes.

HELMER. What a thing to discover! And from you! Whom I adored…whom I worked for! You, who were the whole joy of my life. Lying! That's what it was. Worse than lying—criminal! I tell you, it doesn't seem possible! And yet, I ought to have been prepared for it. I even ought to have foreseen it! Your father had no notion of what principles are…no religion, no morality, no sense of duty! And now look at the way I'm punished for protecting him! Which I did for your sake! And you repay me like this!

> *(Having flung all this at her, he turns to the vestibule doors and closes them, harshly turning back to her to continue his arraignment.)*

You've ruined my future. Do you know that? You've put me square into the hands of a scoundrel; yes, from now on he can do whatever he likes with me—demand what he chooses, domineer over me as much as he likes; and I must submit to everything.

NORA. When I'm out of the world, you'll be free.

HELMER. *(Crossing left, passing her.)* Out of the world? Oh, this is no time for fine phrases! Your father was always ready with them, too. What good would it do if you were out of the world, as you call it? None whatever! He'd blab the story just the same, and people might even suspect me of having been a part of it. Did you ever stop to think of that? They might say that I was at the bottom of it and that I'd egged you on! And it's you I have to thank for all this—you, whom I've petted and spoiled all our married life! Now do you understand what you've done to me?

NORA. Yes.

HELMER. *(Walking past her again, toward the right.)* I just can't believe it… I…look here, this whole thing has got to be straightened out. Take that shawl off. Take it off, I say!

(She doesn't move. He turns and pulls the shawl from her shoulders, flinging it onto the sofa. He is past the first shock now, and is busily looking for a loophole for himself.)

I've got to keep him quiet somehow. That's it. People mustn't find out that there's anything at all out of the way. We'll make things look as though nothing has happened between us. And the children...to think that they've been in your care all this time! I just can't trust them to you. Oh, there's no question of happiness anymore. All I can hope for now is to save what I can, just keep up a show...

(The doorbell rings, stopping him dead.)

Is that the doorbell, as late as this?

*(He takes a tentative step toward the vestibule to answer it, when he sees **ELLEN** come out of the kitchen.)*

Hide, Nora, hide yourself. I'll say you're ill.

*(**ELLEN** returns from the doorway, in the darkened vestibule, and opens the center doors. She is in a nightdress and robe, her hair in braids, her eyes sleepy. She has another familiar blue envelope in her hand.)*

ELLEN. Here's a letter for Mrs. Helmer.

HELMER. *(Trying hard to be casual.)* Who brought it?

ELLEN. I found it under the door.

HELMER. Give it to me.

*(He takes it. **ELLEN** closes the doors and exits to her quarters.)*

HELMER. Yes, it is from him. It's probably the end of us, do you realize that?

(He moves nearer the lamp on the piano, tearing open the envelope, which he drops on the floor. There is a letter inside, and a second piece of paper.)

HELMER. What? Why, Nora, it's your promissory note! *(He reads the letter, his eyes traveling rapidly over the words.)* "Deeply regret that—happy turn in my life has—apologize for"—Oh, God! Nora, I'm saved! I'm saved!

NORA. And I?

HELMER. You, too, yes of course! We're saved, Nora! *(Shaking with relief, he sits on the piano bench beside her, the letter and note in his hand.)* He says… Oh, what does it matter what he says? It's all over! It's finished! I'll tear it up and won't even look at it, the whole thing shall just disappear like a dream!

> *(He tears it into several pieces, rushes to the stove and throws the scraps on the fire. The fire flares up for a moment and, for* **HELMER,** *the* **KROGSTAD** *incident is past.)*

There, it's gone.

> *(Like a man suddenly weak in the knees—and he is—he raises himself up slowly, leaning on the little side table. He takes quite a time to turn toward* **NORA.** *Then:)*

Nora, these must have been three terrible days for you.

NORA. Yes, they have been.

HELMER. Yes, I see now. You did it because you loved me. It was just that you went about it in the wrong way, dear. You didn't have the experience to know how. But the next time, you see, my dearest, you must come to me. Don't you realize that?

> *(***NORA*** looks at him, then looks away again.)*

Nora, you're not going to remember the things I said, are you? Why, the whole world seemed to be falling to pieces around me! It's all going to be forgotten.

NORA. *(With a grave, brief smile.)* Thank you, Thorwald.

> *(She starts for her door.)*

HELMER. What are you going to do?

NORA. Take off my costume.

(She goes into her room, without turning to him, without closing the door.)

HELMER. *(Reaching for the words.)* Yes, dear, that's right. I understand just how you felt. Try to calm down now. There's no need to be frightened anymore. It's all over, and the best thing to do is just not to think about it anymore. You see what I mean, don't you?

(Proceeding methodically to set his physical house in order, while he tries to right himself in **NORA**'*s eyes. He picks up the torn envelope and throws it in the fire.)*

The important thing is that our home is safe, Nora, our beautiful, comfortable home. When you wake up tomorrow, this whole thing we've been through will seem a long way off. Can you hear me, Nora? It will be as though it had never happened. We'll forget all about it.

(He takes **NORA**'*s shawl from the sofa, and neatly folds it, leaving it on the piano.)*

In fact, in a way, I'm glad. I'm glad it happened. We've been through it together and I feel as though you were more mine than ever. I don't see how I could ever have reproached you, because I see now what you had in mind.

(He returns to the bookcase the book **MRS. LINDEN** *had been reading.)*

There, there! No wonder you were frightened, but from now on there'll be nothing to worry about...nothing to worry about...

(He bolts the vestibule doors, and turns slowly as he feels **NORA**'*s presence again in the room. She has changed to a dark street dress and comes from her room carrying a hat and jacket, which she leaves on the chair by the piano.)*

HELMER. Why, what's the matter? Not gone to bed? You've changed your dress?

NORA. Yes, Thorwald, I have changed my dress.

HELMER. But why, when it's so late?

NORA. *(Comes toward him, near the sofas.)* I shall not sleep tonight.

HELMER. Now, Nora, dear...

NORA. *(Sitting on the left-hand sofa.)* It's not so late yet. Sit down, Thorwald.

HELMER. *(Puzzled, he comes toward the other sofa.)* Nora, what do you mean? Your face is so cold and set.

NORA. Sit down, Thorwald.

> *(He does.)*

HELMER. Nora, you frighten me! I don't understand you.

NORA. Yes, that's just it.

> *(He starts to say something.)*

No, don't interrupt me. Listen to what I have to say. We must come to a final settlement, Thorwald.

HELMER. How do you mean?

NORA. Doesn't one thing strike you as we sit here?

HELMER. What are you talking about?

NORA. We've been married eight years. Doesn't it strike you that this is the first time we two have talked together seriously?

HELMER. Seriously? Well, what do you call seriously?

NORA. For eight whole years, ever since the day we first met, we've never exchanged one serious word about serious things.

HELMER. You didn't expect me to trouble you with all sorts of worries you couldn't help me with. After all, a man in business...

NORA. I'm not talking about business. I say that we've never yet tried seriously to get to the heart of anything.

HELMER. *(Asking the question in all honesty.)* My dear child, what have you to do with serious things?

NORA. I have had a great injustice done me, first by my father, then by you, Thorwald.

HELMER. What? By your father and me? We, who have loved you more than all the world?

NORA. Yes, it's so. When I was home with Papa, he used to tell me all his opinions and I agreed with him. If I had others, I kept them to myself, because he wouldn't have liked it. He used to call me his doll-child, and play with me just the way I played with my dolls. Then I came to live in your house...

HELMER. What a way to talk about our marriage!

NORA. I mean I changed hands, from his to yours. So then you settled things according to your taste.

HELMER. Nora!

NORA. I've been living here like a beggar, by performing tricks for you! But that's the way you would have it. You and my father are responsible. It's your fault my life has been wasted.

HELMER. Nora, haven't you been happy here?

NORA. No, never.

HELMER. Not...not happy?

NORA. No, only merry. You've always been kind to me; but our house has been nothing but a nursery. I've been your doll-wife, just as I used to be Papa's doll-child. And, in the same way, my children have been my dolls. That's what our marriage has been, Thorwald.

HELMER. *(Determined to meet this extraordinary argument in some way.)* Well, perhaps there is some truth in what you say, in spite of all your exaggerations. But, Nora, from now on it will be different. Yes, all that playtime is over; now comes the time for education.

NORA. Whose? Mine or the children's?

HELMER. Both, my dear, Nora, both.

NORA. A few minutes ago you said you couldn't trust them to me.

HELMER. But, Nora, I didn't realize what I was saying. I was excited. You mustn't hold that against me.

NORA. Thorwald, I'm leaving you.

HELMER. What are you saying?

NORA. I cannot stay with you.

HELMER. You've lost your mind. I shan't allow it! *(He strikes the table suddenly, then rises.)* Do you hear? I forbid it!

NORA. Neither now, nor in the future am I going to accept anything from you.

HELMER. *(Sitting down again.)* Nora, let's talk about this reasonably and calmly. In the first place, where do you suppose you're going?

NORA. Tomorrow I'm going home.

HELMER. Home?

NORA. To what used to be my home.

HELMER. And what do you propose to do there?

NORA. I'll find an opening.

HELMER. What sort of an opening? Have you had any experience?

NORA. I'll get experience.

HELMER. You mean that you propose to leave your home, your husband, and your children? And have you considered what people will say?

NORA. I don't care what they say.

HELMER. But, Nora, you can't run away from your duties, they're sacred!

NORA. *(So far out of reach of this shibboleth now she doesn't even hear.)* What?

HELMER. Are you trying to infuriate me? Your duties to your husband and your children!

NORA. I don't believe that anymore. From now on I must think things out for myself.

HELMER. Must you think out your place in your own home? Have you no religion?

NORA. I don't know, Thorwald, I really don't know.

HELMER. Well, then what about your conscience? I suppose you have some moral feeling. Answer me! Have you or haven't you?

NORA. That's not easy to say, Thorwald. I really don't know. I hear that laws aren't at all what I thought they were, and I can't believe that they're right.

HELMER. *(Getting up angrily and striding to the center of the room.)* You talk like a child, think like a child! You don't understand the...the whole society in which you live.

NORA. No, I don't.

HELMER. Nora, you're ill, you're feverish! I almost think you're out of your senses.

NORA. I've never felt so clear or so certain.

HELMER. Clear and certain enough to forsake your husband and children?

NORA. Yes.

HELMER. *(Crossing behind her, right.)* Then there's only one possible explanation. You don't love me anymore.

NORA. Yes, that's just it.

HELMER. Nora, what did you say?

NORA. *(It is almost difficult for her to say this necessary thing.)* I'm very sorry, you've always been kind to me, but I can't help it. I don't love you anymore.

HELMER. You're clear and certain of that, too?

NORA. Yes. That's why I can't stay in this house.

HELMER. *(Sitting down again.)* And can you explain to me at what moment you ceased to love me?

NORA. Yes, I can. It was this evening, when the miracle that I expected to happen, didn't happen. It was then I saw that you were not the man I had imagined.

HELMER. Explain yourself more clearly. I don't understand you!

NORA. For eight years now I've been waiting for a certain wonderful thing to happen, to happen between you and me. I've been waiting patiently because I know that really wonderful things can't happen every day. And when I saw that this...this catastrophe was hanging over me, I said to myself, "It's coming—the miracle is coming!"

HELMER. When was this?

NORA. Thorwald, when Krogstad's letter was lying in the box, it never occurred to me that you would think for a minute of submitting to that man's conditions! I was certain that you'd say to him. "All right, tell everybody! Publish it to the whole world!" And I was certain, that after that...

HELMER. After that, what? When I'd covered my wife's name with shame and disgrace?

NORA. Then I was sure you'd come forward and take the whole thing on yourself. You'd say, "I'm the guilty one!"

HELMER. I? But, Nora, you...

NORA. Oh, I'd never have accepted such a sacrifice. Of course not! But what would my word have been against yours? That was the miracle I hoped for, and dreaded. And to prevent that, I wanted to die.

HELMER. Nora, I would gladly work day and night for you, I'd bear any sorrows and want; but no man sacrifices his honor even for the woman he loves!

NORA. Millions of women have done it.

HELMER. *(Exasperated beyond endurance, he rises, crosses center.)* You talk like a child, you think like a child!

NORA. When you got over being frightened—not for me, but for yourself! And you knew there was nothing more to fear, then it was as if nothing had happened! I was your doll again, and you would take twice as much care of it in the future, because I was so weak and fragile. Thorwald, it burst on me in that moment that I had been living here these eight years with a strange man, and had borne him two children. Oh, I can't bear to think of it! I could tear myself to pieces!

HELMER. *(Very still, he's been reached at last.)* I see. I see what's happened. A great gulf has opened up between us. But, Nora, isn't it possible that...*(He comes to her, kneeling beside her, holding her.)* Nora, we can't be torn apart like this!

NORA. *(Heedless of his arms around her, she rises.)* I'm going, Thorwald.

HELMER. *(Getting up from his knees, but still clinging to her.)* Nora, not now! Wait till tomorrow!

NORA. *(She shakes her head and moves away from him.)* I can't spend the night in a strange man's house.

> *(She rises, then walks to the nursery door. She firmly closes it.)*

No, I won't go in to the children. I know they're in better hands than mine.

HELMER. But you're my wife, now and always!

NORA. Thorwald, when a wife leaves her husband's house, as I am doing, I've heard that in the eyes of the law, he is free from all duties to her. *(She comes down to him, with something in her hand.)* At all events, I release you from all duties to me. Here's your ring, give me mine.

> *(She puts her wedding ring in his hand and waits patiently while he blindly pulls off his, compelled by her deep seriousness.*
>
> *All this time she has had her keys in her hand. She gives them to him.)*

Here are the keys. *(She moves to the piano to get her jacket and hat.)* Tomorrow, when I've left town, Christina will come and pack up the things I brought from home.

> *(She puts on her hat, glancing briefly in the mirror. She puts on her jacket, buttoning it against the winter night.)*

I'll have them sent after me.

HELMER. *(Stunned, pleading to her in a low voice.)* Is everything over? Nora, will you never think of me again?

NORA. *(Starting toward the vestibule doors, smiling at him.)* Thorwald, I shall often think of you, and the children, and this house.

> *(She passes him; he can only turn helplessly after her.)*

HELMER. May I write to you, Nora?

NORA. No, never. You mustn't.

HELMER. But I must send you...

NORA. Never, never...

HELMER. But if ever you should need help, I must be the one who...

NORA. *(She unbolts the vestibule doors, opens them.)* No, no, I say...

HELMER. *(Coming toward her.)* Can I never be anything more than a stranger to you?

NORA. Oh, Thorwald, for that...the miracle would have to happen!

HELMER. What's that?

NORA. Both of us would have to change so...that...*(She shakes her head and walks into the dark hall.)* But I no longer believe in miracles.

> *(She opens the outer door.)*

HELMER. *(Coming into the vestibule after her.)* Nora! Nora!

NORA. *(Out of sight now, only a voice, leaving.)* Thorwald, good-bye!

> *(She shuts the door. In a moment the street door is heard to slam and she is gone.)*

> *(His last hopeless cry; he is quite out of sight of the audience, and the room, his house, his whole life, is emptied:)*

HELMER. Nora!

> *(The curtain slowly falls.)*

End of Play

THORNTON WILDER

Thornton Wilder (1897–1975) was a pivotal figure in the literary history of the twentieth-century. He is the only writer to win Pulitzer Prizes for both fiction and drama. He received the Pulitzer for his novel The Bridge of San Luis Rey (1927) and the plays Our Town (1938) and The Skin of Our Teeth (1942). His other best-selling nov¬els include The Cabala, The Woman of Andros, Heaven's My Destination, The Ides of March, The Eighth Day and Theophilus North. His other major dramas include The Matchmaker (adapted as the musical Hello, Dolly!) and The Alcestiad. The Happy Journey to Trenton and Camden, Pullman Car Hiawatha and The Long Christmas Dinner are among his well-known shorter plays.

Wilder's many honors include the Gold Medal for Fiction from the American Academy of Arts and Letters, the Presidential Medal of Freedom, the National Book Committee's Medal for Literature and the Goethe-Plakette Award (Germany).

Wilder was born in Madison, Wisconsin, on April 17, 1897. He spent part of his boyhood in China and was educated principally in California, graduating from Berkeley High School in 1915. After attending Oberlin College for two years, he transferred to Yale, where he received his BA in 1920. His post-graduate studies included a year spent studying archaeology and Italian at the American Academy in Rome (1920-21) and graduate work in French at Princeton (Master's degree, 1926).

In addition to his talents as a playwright and novelist, Wilder was an accomplished essayist, translator, research scholar, teacher, lecturer, librettist and screenwriter. In 1942, he teamed with Alfred Hitchcock on the classic psycho-thriller *Shadow of a Doubt*. Versed in foreign languages, he translated and adapted plays by Ibsen, Sartre and Obey. He read and spoke German, French and Spanish, and his scholarship included significant research on James Joyce and Lope de Vega. Wilder enjoyed acting and played major roles in several of his plays in summer theater productions. He also possessed a lifelong love of music and wrote librettos for two operas based on *The Long Christmas Dinner* (composer Paul Hindemith) and *The Alcestiad* (composer Louis Talma). One of Wilder's deepest passions wasteaching. Hebegan this career in 1921 as an instructor in French at The Lawrenceville School in New Jersey.

During the 1930s he taught courses in Classics in Translation and Composition at the University of Chicago. In 1950–51, he served as the

Charles Eliot Norton Professor of Poetry at Harvard. During WWII, Wilder served in Army Air Force Intelligence. He was awarded the Legion of Merit Bronze Star, the Legion d'honneur and the Order of the British Empire.

In 1930, with royalties received from *The Bridge of San Luis Rey*, Wilder built a home for himself and his family in Hamden, Connecticut. Although often away from home, up to as many as 250 days a year, restlessly seeking quiet places in which to write, he always returned to "The House that the Bridge Built." He died here on December 7, 1975.

HENRIK IBSEN (1828–1906) was a nineteenth-century Norwegian playwright, poet and theater director. He is often considered the father of modern realism. Ibsen was born in the small town of Skien, Norway, in 1828, to a rich merchant family. When he was a child his family fell into financial ruin—themes that Ibsen would later explore in many of his works, most notably *Peer Gynt*. His other plays include *A Doll's House* (1879), *Hedda Gabbler* (1891), *An Enemy of the People* (1882), *The Master Builder* (1892), *The Wild Duck* (1884) and *Ghosts* (1881). Ibsen is the second most produced dramatist in the world after William Shakespeare. He died in 1906.